SUDDEN IMPACT

SUDDEN IMPACT

Clyde Braden

NORTH STAR PRESS OF ST. CLOUD, INC.

Saint Cloud, Minnesota

ISBN: 0-87839-444-3
ISBN-13: 978-0-87839-444-9

First Edition, September 2011

Printed in the United States of America

Published by
North Star Press of St. Cloud, Inc.
P.O. Box 451
St. Cloud, Minnesota 56302

www.northstarpress.com

1 2 3 4 5 6 7 8 9 10

SUDDEN IMPACT

CHAPTER ONE

S LOWLY, BEECHCRAFT BONANZA, LICENSE number 3211V boldly identifying itself in bright white over red, lifted off the runway and climbed away from the airport to cruising altitude. Brian "Scotty" Mac-Tavish changed his radio to Chicago Control frequency, and called, "Chicago Control, this is Bonanza three two one one victor."

"One victor, Chicago Control."

"Chicago Control, please activate my flight plan. Pilot is Brian Mac-Tavish, off the ground at 09:35 VFR (visual flight regulations) direct to Minneapolis Flying Cloud Field. Estimated flight time, two hours thirty-five minutes. One victor, clear."

"Roger, one victor, flight plan activated. Chicago, clear."

Ten minutes later, Nancy Gillett, the owner of Gillette Flight Service who had tried to talk him out of this flight, invaded his concerns for his critically ill young son. "Bonanza three two one one victor, this is Gillette Flight Service."

"Go ahead, Nancy."

"Scotty, fog is forming here. This is a fast moving weather system. It could overrun you before you see it coming. I recommend you return or set down wherever you can."

"Thanks for the warning, Nancy, but I'll keep going. I've got a good start and a light tail wind. I can make it before the weather catches up to me. As I told you, I must get back home today. My first-born son, Billy, is very sick. My wife, Grace, shouldn't have to do this alone. I have to be there to support my wife and son. One victor is clear."

Scotty tuned in the Rockford Omni navigation beacon and set the autopilot to "home," on the beacon. He plugged a cassette into the tape machine and let Tchaikovsky's "Symphony #6 in B Minor" float through the cockpit. The music of the one-hundred-eighty horsepower Continental engine was singing its single note just under Tchaikovsky's Sixth. He let the combined music of Tchaikovsky and the Continental engine flood his senses and relax his mind and body. It was a wonderfully natural sound. He was happy, all things considered.

The peace and solitude of flying alone was something he always enjoyed, especially when there was music in the background. The air was smooth; in fact it was unusually smooth, even for winter, and the sun was shining. Small puffy clouds floated by the cockpit. He noted the passing of the outbound Rockford Illinois Omni navigation beacon. With some effort, he brought himself back to reality, disengaged the autopilot, and altered his heading for the inbound leg to Minneapolis and re-engaged the autopilot.

He took the time to calculate the ground speed for his outbound leg. He was surprised. His ground speed wasn't as fast as it should have been. Maybe the wind had changed. He listened to the weather briefing from Rockford. Yes, the upper winds had died to nothing. It also told him the fog was, indeed, moving fast. In fact, it was moving faster than he could fly. He looked down and saw a thick, unbroken undercast.

A twisted smile moved across Scotty's face. "Damn, Nancy was right. I'll never live this down. Maybe I can still make Flying Cloud before it closes."

He ejected the cassette from the tape drive and began paying more attention to what was happening around him. As he moved closer to the Twin Cities, he continued to listen to enroute weather. He wasn't hearing what he wanted so desperately to hear.

Scotty let his mind float back in time to when he had first met the owner of Gillett Flight Service. It was the day he flew into Chicago to interview for a ferry pilot position with Aircraft Unlimited. He had flown in from Minneapolis in an old Cessna 150. *Now she tells me not to fly back to Minnesota with the Bonanza because she feels heavy fog will overrun me. She knows the Bonanza isn't equipped for instrument flying. I should have listened. But, I had to get back. Billy and Grace need me there. If I develop a head wind I could have a fuel problem. If I make Flying Cloud, I won't have much reserve fuel*, he thought.

Scotty wasn't really that nervous about bringing the Bonanza through the clouds. He had practiced a blind descent on many occasions. He just couldn't do an instrument approach to the runway. As long as he had a hundred feet of vertical distance and at least three hundred feet for horizontal vision, he was confident of making a safe landing. He could ask for a tower controlled direction approach and let down through the fog.

When he was twenty miles away from Flying Cloud, he found out the field had closed to all VFR traffic. At that time the ceiling had dropped to fifty feet with horizontal visibility at less than two-hundred feet. Scotty looked at the guilty fuel gauge, switching it to the left wing tank. It was empty. The right wing tank, had less than a quarter left. He switched to the auxiliary tank, also empty. He could see a serious problem developing. That right wing tank was too close to empty. He switched the fuel gauge to read the auxiliary tank a second time. It still indicated empty.

Scotty had a habit of using his auxiliary tank up first. His reason was that it would require filling after every flight. That way he always knew the fuel in that tank would be fresh. That's not what most pilots did.

Now what do I do? I better report this to flight service. Boy, Len will give me a bad time about this. I can remember him telling me over and over again that there's no possible excuse for running out of fuel. With that thought he switched the radio frequency. "Minneapolis Flight Service, Bonanza three two one one victor."

"Minneapolis, go ahead one victor."

"Minneapolis, could you give me current weather and location of the nearest airport still open to VFR."

"One victor, Alexandria is the closest airfield still open but their weather is deteriorating fast."

"Minneapolis, please change my flight plan to Alexandria. I would like to inform you of a short fuel problem. This trip has taken more time then I had planned. I'll probably arrive at Alex with dry tanks."

"Roger, one victor. Situation noted. Good luck. Minneapolis out."

Heading for Alexandria, another hundred plus miles, at the most economical engine setting, he hoped it would stay open long enough for him to land. He knew most of the people in the flight service station there. He could ask them to use their direction finding (D.F.) equipment to vector him to the airfield, if it becomes necessary. It would be quicker for them to guide him, then for him to grope around trying to find the runway.

Scotty's thoughts drifted again to Nancy. Her words echoed in his mind. *Why do you think you need to fly back today? The weather's turning sour and you know it. That beautiful old Bonanza you're flying, you're pride and joy, doesn't deserve to die because you're in a hurry to get home to that bride and son of yours, even if he is sick. What good are you to them if you're dead?*

You might be instrument rated but that plane isn't. It has one radio and no instrumentation. If that radio goes bad, you're deaf, dumb, blind and probably dead. If an undercast forms, how the hell are you going to get through it in one piece?

"*Boy did she give me an earful. But, I guess I deserved it,*" Scotty thought. At thirty miles out, he picked up his microphone and called, "Alexandria, this is Bonanza three two one one victor."

"Go ahead, one victor."

"Alexandria, I'm thirty miles out, VFR, on top and running low on fuel. What is your status?"

"One victor, Scotty, if that's you, we're closed to all traffic except IFR, and that could change at any time. The weather's really lousy here and it's getting worse by the minute."

"Willy, I've got a little problem here. My fuel gauge has been resting on the empty peg for the past four minutes. I need to get under this stuff and find the field, quickly. I'll declare an emergency. Could you give me a D.F. heading?"

"Sure we can, but are you sure you can reach the field? We wouldn't want you to come up short and find a building in your way."

"It's a moot point now, my friend. The engine just shut down. All three of my tanks are dry. I'm ten minutes out and currently on a heading of two hundred seventy-five degrees. I don't know what's under me, but I'll find out. Man, I hope it's soft. Scramble the crash crew, Willy. I think I'm going to get very busy in the next few minutes. See you soon. One victor clear."

William Slocum pulled a pad of emergency reports in front of him. He looked at the clock. It was exactly 3:52 p.m. He picked up his phone and reported the crash of, Beechcraft Bonanza 3211V piloted by Brian MacTavish. Then he began filling out the written report.

When Scotty broke out of the thick fog, a wispy fog remained, allowing him some horizontal visibility. He had hoped to see one of the many frozen lakes around Alexandria. No such luck. If he could have found one, he would have been able to land with wheels down and saved the plane and himself a lot of trouble.

What he did see was the tops of trees rushing past his wings. He was, maybe, thirty feet above the highest of them. That was closer then he wanted to be. Quickly, he scanned the horizon for a clearing big enough to use. He saw nothing but treetops, not even a dirt road was visible. He had a little speed to work with but not much.

Wait—is that a small clearing? Yes! Yes, it is. Hard left turn. Easy now. Don't stall it. Line up with the best angle. Man, is that short. I hope I can make it. Got to get the set-up perfect the first time. I can't go around for another try. I'll need to land on the belly, so gear up, power switch off—losing altitude too fast. I'm getting too close to the treetops.

Oh, man, this is going to be closer than I want—NO! I'm going into the trees—full flaps—control the balloon—great, just enough to clear the trees. Nose down—do a smooth flare—now slow down as much as you can—set it down easy—easy—easy—don't let it hit hard, get set.

Scotty felt a soft bump and the nose came up a little, and then he hit the ground and began sliding toward the tree line. He hit something in his path that threw the plane a little off the straight line he had hoped to maintain. The tail of the plane came up high and as it did, he put his hands on the cabin ceiling and pushed back into the seat. He thought it would flip over but at the last minute, it dropped back with a hard thump and continued sliding toward the trees at a high rate of speed.

The tree line began getting larger much faster then he wanted. The warm temperatures earlier in the day had melted the snow enough to form a hard ice crust after the fog layer cooled the rays of the sun. The grinding noises he heard suggested he had broken through the crust but he still wasn't slowing down fast enough.

"Oh, my God, I'm going to hit the trees head-on. Grace, I'm sorry. I made a terrible mistake and I'm going to die for it! I love you. Don't let Billy forget me." He crossed his arms over his face just as the first trees passed the nose of the bonanza and then a loud tearing sound as the wings ripped off and the fuselage continued forward until it plowed into a snow drift and came to a sudden stop. Scotty's head snapped forward violently, and then everything went black.

CHAPTER TWO

BILL MACTAVISH CALLED TO HIS FIFTEEN-YEAR-OLD SON, "Brian, where are you heading? Supper's almost ready and your mother wants you to come in and wash your hands."

Brian rode his bike back into the yard and parked it by the back steps. He looked up at his father, "I was, just, going over to the airfield to watch the planes, Dad, but I can do that after supper," he answered.

Bill shook his head. For the past three years he hadn't been able to understand the fascination his son had with airplanes. He spent most of his free time at the airfield, summer and winter. In fact, ever since they had bought him the bike.

"May I be excused?" Brian asked when he had cleaned his plate.

Bill nodded his head and said, "Yes, you may. Please be back before dark. Remember tomorrow is a school day."

"I remember. Thanks, Dad." He got up from the table, took his dishes to the sink, rinsed them off and stacked them in the sink. He sauntered towards the back door and walked out, carefully closing the door so it wouldn't slam.

He biked a mile to the airfield and turned in the gravel drive past the sign that pointed to BOERGER FLIGHT SERVICE Flying Lessons and Air Charter. He leaned his bike against a tree alongside the back entrance, walked in the back door and said, "Hi," to the lady behind the counter and then went out the front door.

He moved to one side of the entrance and sat on the ground. There were two planes circling the airfield. One would land and immediately take off again. Then the second would do the same thing. Len Boerger, the owner, chief pilot, and flying instructor had told him about that maneuver. It was called, "a touch and go landing." It was used to practice take-off and landings. It sure looked like fun.

All he could think of was learning to fly. For the next few years, all of his actions and desires were aimed at one end. Being able to fly a plane and getting his pilot's license.

Len had told him if he finished the ninth grade with high marks he would give him a par-time job to help pay for lessons. He would have to do everything Len told him and in the order he specified. Len said if he did everything correctly, he would help him to be a good pilot.

He would graduate from ninth grade in a few weeks. So far, his grades were very good. His last report card had five A's and one B. Of course that "B" had to be in his English class. He had worked hard since then to bring that B up to an A. That should satisfy Len. At least he hoped it would. He just had to learn to fly.

He kept his eye on the prize. His resolve to graduate ninth grade at the top of his class was very real.

Friday, the day of school finals arrived with bright sunshine and warm temperatures. Brian woke up well rested and full of confidence. He knew he would do well. He was ready. By the end of the day, he was even more confident of his chances. He hadn't found a single question he didn't know the answer to. Now, he would have to wait six days before he would get his report card.

Bill MacTavish took his son fishing at a lake in the northern part of the state. Fishing was the only thing that could get Brian's mind off flying.

Monday morning, Brian went back to school. As the day slowly wore on, he went through the motions of trying to pay attention. It was a lost cause. His mind was high in the sky and he couldn't get it to come down. All of the tests were finished and all he wanted was his report card so he could get on with his flying lessons.

After school, Brian rode the bus home. He stopped in long enough to change his clothes and say goodbye to his mother. He slipped out the back door and picked up his bike and peddled down the road toward the airport.

Len and his wife, Barbara, were behind the counter when he walked in. "When do you want me to start working, Mr. Boerger? Brian asked.

"Let's see your report card?" Len responded.

"I won't get it until Thursday, but I'm confident it will be a good one. I just wanted to know when I should plan on being here. I don't want to waste any time."

"If he's that confident Len, give him a start date so he can plan his time. I think he'll satisfy even a hard nose like you." Barbara said.

"All right, if your report card is good enough on Thursday, and you have your parent's permission, you can start at six o'clock Saturday morning. I want to see that report card on Thursday though. I don't want to see anything less than a 'B.' Do you understand?" Len asked.

Brian's face broke out in a smile and he quipped, "Mr. Boerger, you have a new employee and a new student." He walked out the door to the ramp and sat down to watch the planes taking off and landing.

"He's a cocky kid. I sure hope he's as good as he thinks he is," Len said.

"Give him a chance. He isn't much different from you at that age. From what your mother told me you could have been brothers," Barbara said grinning.

He gave her a "Harrumph" and walked out the side door to the hanger. He began to mumble to himself, "I'll make sure he's a competent pilot. If he has any talent at all, he will make himself a good pilot. I'll start him in ground school for the first year or so. Then I'll get him into the air. By the time he graduates from high school he could have his private license."

Len's thoughts brought his mind back to when he learned to fly. His teacher didn't have safety in mind when he taught. Len still thinks about his crash and how lucky he had been. He didn't want that to happen to this kid. *Barb's right. Brian does remind me of myself,* he thought.

Len rolled the Cherokee Six out of the hanger. It had more leg room and a much quieter cabin. He had a short charter flight to do this evening. When he carried people, he liked to use that airplane because it was more comfortable for the passengers. He did a slow walk around pre-flight check of the plane. *If I had done this with the Piper Cub, I never would have gone down. Yup, I'll teach young Brian caution and safety first. That way he has a good chance of staying out of the kind of troubles I had,* he thought.

Brian sat in the late afternoon sunshine, watching and listening to everything that was going on. Time seemed to stand still. He couldn't get enough. The sun was getting low on the horizon when he looked at the clock inside the line office. He jumped up, ran around the building, grabbed his bike, and peddled for home.

He ran in the back door of the house, hoping his dad would be late getting home. He wasn't, there he was sitting at the kitchen table. But there wasn't any food on the table yet.

Brian ran into the bathroom and washed his hands. He came back into the kitchen and slid into his chair just as his mother put the first serving dish on the table. Kim screwed up her face in a frown and whined, "You're late."

"That's cutting it a little close isn't it, son?" Bill asked.

"Yes, sir, I did cut it too close. I'll do better." Brian answered.

Supper went quietly. Brian's mother and dad talked of household things. Brian kept thinking about Len's requirement of his parent's permission to work at the airport. He didn't know how he would get them to give their permission. He decided the direct approach would be the best. He would talk with them right after the dishes were finished.

While he and Kim were washing the dishes, Brian talked with his mother. "I've been thinking, a lot, about what I want to do with my life. Mom, I would like to learn to fly an airplane. If I can, I think I would like to be an airline pilot."

Mae, with a sad smile on her face and the look of stark fear in her eyes, looked at her son. "I'm afraid that's out of the question, at least right now. We just can't afford flying lessons. Besides you're too young yet, maybe when you finish high school."

"I know you can't afford to buy lessons for me, and yes, I am too young right now, but when I am old enough, I want to be ready to take the test. I have a solution to both objections and I'd like to talk with you and dad about it as soon as we finish dishes. Would that be all right?"

"Well, we're almost finished. We'll talk to your father about it. Why don't you go in and find out if he has time to talk with us," she said.

To his surprise, Kim hadn't said a word. He thought she would have put up a big argument. He didn't want to make her mad so he said, "No, I'll stay and finish. Then, we can all go in."

At this moment, Mae told Brian quietly and with some caution in her voice. "Being an airline pilot is very dangerous. When a plane crashes, the pilot is always killed. I don't want my son in any kind of dangerous profession. After all, Brian, you're our only son. At the same time, I want you to challenge yourself. You are an intelligent young man who has never given us any problems. I want you to make your own decisions, but with some guidance from the family."

They finished the dishes and Mae swept the floor while Brian put the dishes away and Kim rinsed out the sink. Then they all went into the living room. Bill was sitting in the overstuffed 1920s wing chair, reading the paper. Mae looked at Brian then turned to Bill and said, "Bill, Brian has something he wants to talk with us about. Do you have time to do it now?"

Bill looked up from his paper, folded it, and put it on his lap. "Of course I do. What is it, Brian? Are you afraid of some bad grades after your finals?"

"No, Dad, my grades are fine. I'm hoping for all A's this time. What I wanted to talk about is a part-time job I can get, with permission from both of you. I want to get my pilot's license and eventually become an airline pilot."

Bill started to say something, but Brian continued quickly, "I know you and mom can't afford lessons for me, and yes, I'm too young right now but I want to be ready and have the necessary knowledge when I'm old enough."

"That's a good profession but are you sure that's what you want? It takes a lot of money and a lot of study and work to become an airline pilot. That could take many years past high school. At the very least four years at college, plus all of the flight training. Are you sure you want to devote all that time to that kind of career?" Bill asked.

"I'm not committed to the airlines yet. All I know is, I want to learn to fly. That's what this part-time job is about. Mr. Boerger has offered me a job at his flight service in exchange for helping me get a pilot's license." Brian answered.

"What are his requirements? What are you going to be doing? How much are you going to be making? How many hours are you working? And, how does he intend to handle your age situation?" Bill asked.

"I don't know if I can answer all of your questions. His requirements are good grades, nothing below a B, and I need my parent's permission. I'm not sure what I'll be doing or how much I'll make. We haven't talked about that yet. Mr. Boerger said he wanted to talk with the both of you and me. He said I could start learning right now but I couldn't take the flight test until my eighteenth birthday. That would be just before I graduate."

"I don't know, Brian," his dad said.

Brian pleaded, "Please, Dad. My grades are good. I promise to keep them up. Even if they drop, I'll lose my job at the airport. Please, Dad, let me try. I want to do this so bad."

"When does he want to see us?" Mae asked.

"I get my report card Thursday. That's the last day of school. I can start working Saturday morning," he answered.

Bill looked at Mae, he said, "Tell Mr. Boerger we'll be over to see him at seven o'clock Thursday evening. Provided your grades fall within his guidelines."

Brian's face lit up like a spring sunrise. "Thanks, Dad. Thanks, Mom." He gave each of them a big hug, ran out the back door, being careful not to let it slam, jumped on his bike and set out for the airport.

When he arrived, he found Len wasn't back from his charter. Len's wife was behind the counter. He told her that he would be back with his mother and father at seven o'clock Thursday evening. He would have his report card with him. Barbara looked in her appointment book to see if the time was clear. It was. She wrote his name in the book.

He knew his report card would be all right and now he was sure his parents would give their permission. He would be on his way Saturday morning. "Wow, it's getting late. I'd better get home." He straddled his bike and pointed it up the gravel road toward home. He parked his bike alongside the back porch and walked in the back door.

Brian noted the family car was gone. When he looked around the house, he couldn't find his mother or father. *Maybe they went shopping,* he thought.

He went up to his room and turned on his radio. He found some quiet music and turned it down low. He lay back on his bed to think and dream about someday flying into the sky on a bright sunny day, in a beautiful new airplane all by himself. It was a heady daydream, but one he intended to make come true.

"Brian, can I come in? I'd like to talk to you." Kim said.

Brian snapped back to reality, "I thought you had gone with the folks. Sure come in. What's up?"

"First, I hope Mom and Dad let you take this job. I hope you get to fly someday. Maybe you'll take me for a ride after you get your license. I know I've been giving you a hard time for the past few years, but that's my job. I'm your little sister. I'm supposed to give you a hard time. It's part of my job description. Little sisters of brilliant big brothers need to bring them down to earth once in a while. I can still be proud of my big brother, can't I?"

"Okay, Kimberly, what do you want?" Brian said.

"Just a little brotherly advice is all," she said.

"That sounds serious, Kim. What's the problem?" Brian asked.

"Jack Stubblefield is the problem," she said. "Please don't tell Mom and Dad about this. You know I've been dating Jack for a few weeks now."

"Yes, I do, Kim. You're only thirteen years old. I also know the folks don't want you dating yet. If I were you, I'd be very careful about where you go with him. He's at least three years older than you and has a reputation for getting his girl friends pregnant."

"That's what I'm afraid of," she said. Brian started to get off the bed. Kim raised both hands and said, "Wait a minute, big brother. Nothing has happened between us—yet. He's been trying to get me to go all the way with him. He's tried to put his hands on me, but I wouldn't let him. He wants me to go to a drive-in movie with him tonight. I've tried to tell him I couldn't go, but he said I was going with him whether I wanted to or not. My question is how I can get out of going."

"When is he coming over to get you?" Brian asked.

"In about fifteen minutes," she said.

"Okay, when he gets here, you stay in the house. I'll go out and talk with him."

"Thanks, big brother," she said.

Brian watched his sister walk out of the room. Now he saw something he hadn't seen before. *My little sister is becoming a beautiful young woman.*

He muttered under his breath, "No wonder Jack is trying to get into her pants. She's a cute chick." *How did this happen so fast? I'll have to keep an eye on my little sister for the next few years,* he thought.

Brian heard the *horn honk* outside. He got up, walked outside and got into the car with Jack. They talked for about five minutes, Brian got out of the car, and Jack drove away.

When he came back into the house, Kim commented, "I've never seen Jack drive so careful. What did you tell him?"

"I asked him if you had ever said anything about our family. He said you hadn't. So I told him our mother was Italian, and was connected to the boys in Chicago. I told him that Mom didn't want you dating yet. I told him if he was smart he would wait a few years because if Mom knew what was going on, she would tell her brothers, and Jack would be a very sorry young man."

They both laughed and Kim punched her brother and said, "Thanks a lot."

At last, Thursday morning arrived. He went to his homeroom. From there, he went to the auditorium for a program, then back to his homeroom just before noon. The report cards were handed out and he was free for the summer.

He met Kim on the bus. She said she had seen Jack, and he had been as sweet as pie.

"Kim, please don't tease Jack or any other guy. You'll get a reputation as a tease and one day you'll be gang raped. That won't be fun. Wait until you're ready for a serious affair, then go for it."

"Okay, Brian. I'll do the best I can," she responded. "Let me see your report card."

Brian handed it to her. She looked and squealed, "You did it. Straight A's! Do I have a great brother, or what?"

He changed his mind about going to the airport. His parents needed to see the report card first. When everyone was seated at the table, Brian passed his report card to his father. Bill looked it over and commented, "Good job, son." He passed it over to Mae.

She looked at it very carefully. A shiver of fear passed through her heart and she quickly pushed it away. She forced a weak smile and looked into his eyes. "Wonderful, Brian," she said and passed the report card back to him.

Supper went very slowly. The dishes were washed and dried and they had fifteen minutes to get to their meeting with Len Boerger. Brian was on pins and needles but they finally left.

Brian introduced his parents to Len and they moved into Len's office. When everyone was seated Len said, "I think Brian's told you something of my offer. Let me explain just what I have in mind for him and how I would like to handle it. If you have any questions, just ask."

He continued, "Brian is a sharp young man who likes airplanes. He wants to be a pilot. Okay, I can help him reach that goal. But that's not all I want him to learn. Anyone can learn how to steer a plane and make it go up and down. That's not what I want Brian to be. I want him to know what an airplane is, what it does, why it does it, and what happens when something goes wrong. I can teach him to fly, but if he's serious about making this a career, I want him to go to college and learn everything he can about flight."

"We want the same thing. I'm not sure if a flying career is what's best for him, but we're willing to listen," Bill stated.

"At least we agree that Brian needs a college education. We can help there also. Here's what I propose: This summer, I'll pay him four dollars an hour to sweep up the office, keep the hanger floor clean, dry, and fuel aircraft. I'll keep three dollars out of every four in an account, to pay for training. The first year will be ground school. He'll be learning about airplanes and the theory of flight. Then we'll take up weather and how it affects an airplane. Next comes all phases of navigation including electronic navigation and dead reckoning. The last part will be Federal Aviation Regulation or FAR's as we call them. When he has all that down, he'll need to pass a flight physical, and then he can take the test for his student license," Len said promptly.

"If he passes that test he'll be able to start duel flight instruction, stressing safety as well as competence. We'll also move him up to six dollars an hour with four dollars being kept for training. He'll start learning the nuts and bolts of an aircraft, working with me, and Buster, my A and E (airframe and engine) mechanic, as an apprentice. There will be a lot of books to study as well as practical experience. Somewhere in the second year, I hope he'll be able to take his test for airframe mechanic. If he does, his wages will be raised accordingly. By that time, he'll have soloed and will be able to fly alone. He will still have a student license. No passengers will be allowed, except a licensed flight instructor." Bill and Mae listened closely as Len continued.

"After he gets his airframe license, he'll be studying power plants, both internal combustion and the new jet engines. He'll still be working as a mechanic but now it will be with engines as well as airframes. I'm not a licensed engine mechanic but Buster is."

Mae tentatively asked, "Isn't that an a great amount of studying? I'm afraid Brian won't be able to keep up at school. And even if he does, he won't have any social life at all. Isn't that what being a young person is all about, to learn how to socialize with other people?"

"You're right in asking those questions. Brian knows he must maintain a high grade point average at school or the deal is off. As for the social aspect, he'll be in daily contact with people who are well-educated, friendly and in many cases rich. These contacts will never hurt a young person's future. I hope that has answered your question. But, let me continue.

"Flight instructions will be cross-country, navigation, and instrumentation. By his eighteenth birthday he'll be ready to take his flight test. When that's complete, I want him to start on his instrument and commercial ratings. By that time he will be not only a good pilot, but a safe one. He'll know what makes an airplane tick and know how to wind up one that has stopped ticking. It'll give him a leg up on everyone else if he decides to go for a degree in aeronautical engineering. If he doesn't go that direction, it will give him a running start anywhere in the industry.

Len took a breath and continued, "And, last but not least, I'll give him a report once a month with total earnings, paid earnings, and cost of training. I think that just about sums it up. Any further questions?"

"I have one question. Have you ever done this kind of thing before?" Bill asked.

"No, I haven't. Primarily because I've never found anyone that's been sharp enough or interested enough to go through this kind of rigorous training. I'm not going to kid anyone. It will be difficult. Brian will need to keep his school grades up. If that doesn't happen, the whole deal is off and any money I'm holding for training will be turned over to him." Len answered.

"Why are you doing this for Brian?" Mae asked.

"Some of what I want to do with Brian was done for me when I was Brian's age, but the safety aspect and knowledge of how and aircraft worked and why it does, was never stressed. I had to learn those lessons the hard way. I believe in giving back some of what I received. Brian is the first young man who has showed enough intelligence and drive to pull it off. Believe me when I say, it's going to be tough for a few years."

So far Brian hadn't said a word. "What about it, Brian? Do you think you can handle all this?" Len asked.

"All I want to do is learn how to fly and be the best pilot I can be," he said.

"Do you realize that most of your time will be spent going to school and to the airport? That you'll be under extreme pressure to keep your grades up and at the same time, learn a demanding profession like flying?" Mae questioned.

"Yes, I understand that. I want to do it. I will do it. I promise my grades will not go below a B average," he exclaimed.

"Let's talk it over at home so we don't take a lot of Len's time. Brian will get back to you by Friday night," Bill said.

"That sounds like a good idea," Mae said.

"I don't see what the problem is. I want to do it. It's my choice. I'll be the one doing the work and if I fail, it will be over and then you both can say, 'I told you so.' I don't need to think or talk it over. This is what I want to do, and it's what I will do, now or later." Brian said.

Len looked at Brian and said, "The enthusiasm is good, but your parents have your best interest at heart, Brian. I think it would be a good idea for you to talk about the whole program with them. Let them know what you want to do with your life. Show them where you want to be ten years from now. It'll be a lot easier for you, with them on your side."

"I guess you're right," Brian said with a downcast face.

"Good. I'll see you tomorrow. I'll be gone until late afternoon, but I'll see you when I get back," Len said.

Bill, Mae, and Brian left the office. Nobody said a word during the short trip home. When they arrived, the three of them walked slowly into the living room.

After all three had taken seats, Brian said, "I don't know what's holding up your approval. This is what I want to do. I'll be doing the work and I'll be required to keep my grades up. I want to be a pilot. I want to know how an airplane works. I want to be an airline pilot or some other kind of pilot. I know I can do this. It's the best way for me to get the education you want me to have, and it won't cost you anything."

"I agree with you, Brian. It is a good opportunity to learn about flying, but the stress on you to do well at school and with Len will be great. I just don't want you to hurt yourself. Another thing that really bothers me a great deal is that airplanes are not safe. We have had several airplanes that have crashed just since the first of the year. In all cases, everyone has been killed. I just don't want that to happen to you," Mae said.

"Son, your mother and I just want the best for you. I'm not against this program at all. It sounds like something you could handle but I would want you to go to college, too. If you really intend to be an airline pilot, you'll need to have that college degree or no airline will talk to you about being a pilot, no matter how good you are. Another thing you should keep in mind is the competition for those flying jobs by the military pilots."

"I understand, Dad. College is something I want, too. I'll be more able to put myself through school, and I'll have a big jump on that degree with what I can learn from Mr. Boerger and Buster. That way, you and Mom will be able to send Kim to college, too."

About that time, Kim walked into the room. "Mom, Dad, I think you should let Brian do this. I've been standing outside the room, listening to your discussion. Brian wants this opportunity, very much. He made straight A's in school. He's smart. He can do both at the same time even if I have to help him," she added. "As a reward for his report card, let him do it for the next year. If he's going to screw-up, he'll do it before the end of the year."

Bill and Mae looked at one another, then Bill turned to Brian and said, "Okay, son. You have our permission. However, we want to look at this again at the end of summer vacation."

Brian jumped up and ran to hug both of his parents. "Thanks. You won't be sorry. I'll do the best I can."

He turned to his little sister, hugged her close and said, "I didn't expect any help from you, Kim. Thanks, and thanks for saying you'd help. I may take you up on that."

CHAPTER THREE

SLOWLY, SCOTTY BEGAN TO MOVE. His eyes fluttered and he moaned. His face twisted in pain and he cried out, "Oh, man, I hurt."

His eyes fluttered again and tried to open. His eyes popped open and he quickly looked around the cockpit. His sight was clear but his mind couldn't comprehend.

"Oh, man, my head is slamming like a bass drum. I'm cold—so tired—what's happened? Wait a minute. Something isn't right." Once again he scanned the instrument panel and around the front of the aircraft.

The windshield was broken, the instrument panel didn't look like it was in the right position, and none of the instruments were working.

He turned his head to look out of the side window. He started to realize what had happened. "Oh, shit. Oh, my God, I've crashed. Think. Come on use your head. Where am I? What happened? Why did I crash?"

He moved as though to get out of the plane. He screamed with pain. Dizziness claimed him and he began to retch. He repeated to himself, in mantra fashion. "Relax, Relax, Relax." He closed his eyes and waited for the nausea to subside.

His mind took over again and he began to check himself over. Slowly, he moved his head from side to side. He flexed the fingers on his right hand. He moved his hand, then the whole arm. "Well, that much works," he said to the empty cockpit. He tried to flex the fingers of his left hand. They didn't move. He tried the left arm and cried out, "Ahhhh, damn, that hurt. I won't do that again."

Slowly he continued the inventory of his injuries. Both legs were jammed in place by a crushed instrument panel. He thought, *both legs are probably broken, but for the moment, I can't feel any pain in either of them.* He was bleeding from several head wounds and from his legs. The broken left arm showed blood soaking through his suit coat. He wondered if the bleeding was bad enough that he might be in danger of bleeding to death. For the next few minutes, he worked on those wounds trying to stop the bleeding.

With most of the bleeding stopped, Scotty's energy was now focused on how he would get help. He began talking to himself, to help organize his thoughts. *Why didn't the plane catch fire?"*

He looked around at the cabin again. This time more slowly. He took stock of what he had to work with. "The cockpit seems intact. There are holes in the fuselage skin but I don't see any wires hanging loose. The windshield is spider-webbed but still in the frame." He looked out the side windows, and a movement caught his eye. A smile cracked his face. A white-tailed deer stood watching him from a safe distance. The deer soon lost interest and moved away. The side windows were cracked but still in place and the cabin door looked undamaged. The instrument panel pinned his legs in one position. He needed to get his legs free to find out how badly they were hurt.

Both front seats adjusted vertically as well as fore and aft. To try and free his legs from the instrument panel, Scotty fumbled with his right hand trying to reach the height adjustment lever. He found it and pulled. The seat dropped and slammed all the way back at the same time. He screamed as the collapsed instrument panel ripped at his legs and the bleeding began again.

Wiping the tears from his eyes, he waited for the pain to subside. He looked at the damage to his legs. Not as bad as he first thought. The panel had caused a tear in the skin of one thigh. He ripped a piece of cloth from his shirttail and held pressure to the wound long enough to slow the bleeding. He tied the shirttail dressing onto the wound with a piece of string he found in his map case using his good hand and teeth. It didn't appear to be a deep wound. It should be okay, as long as it didn't start bleeding again.

He tried to move his legs. *Okay, the right leg moves from side to side, but I can't lift it. No movement at all in the left leg. I still don't have feeling in either leg. For now that's probably a good thing, but I'll have to be careful I don't let them get too cold. I'll have to find something to cover them. I can't take a chance of freezing my legs.*

He looked out the side window. The fog, close to the ground looked like it had little tendrils moving across the crusty snow. Through those tendrils he could see about a hundred feet. The fog had moved down to the ground. That wasn't what he needed. From what he could see, he had come down in a small clearing and then slid into the trees.

Large trees were on both sides of his plane, almost close enough to reach out and touch from his seat. He could see the edge of the trees and a portion of the clearing. He hadn't slid in very far, but the fuselage was completely under the trees, making it more difficult for search planes to find him. Besides, in this weather, they wouldn't put search planes up until the fog cleared.

Both wings had been torn off at the fuselage. That explained why there wasn't a fire. He had left the fuel tanks somewhere behind him, inside the severed wings.

The nose of the Bonanza was buried in a snowdrift. He looked at the landing gear lever. It was still in the up position. He must have landed with the wheels up to keep from flipping the plane. That's why he slid so far. How lucky he was. He could have hit those trees dead on the nose. If he had, he wouldn't have survived.

More than anything, he wanted to get out of the plane but his mind told him not to. With no threat of fire, he was better off inside. The Bonanza's cabin was warm for the moment and it would give him some protection from the elements. He had put a lot of insulation into the walls and ceiling.

How am I going to get myself back to civilization? he thought. "If you're going to crash an airplane, Minnesota in January isn't the best time or place to do it."

The temperature must be below freezing because ice crystals were forming on branches and windfalls. Darkness was creeping closer.

"Wow, I never expected something like this to happen. It was a basic, straightforward, two-and-a-half-hour flight home." Scotty let his mind go blank. His eyes closed and he let his head slump to his chest. Almost instantly he was asleep.

Within a few minutes, his eyes fluttered open again, and he began talking to himself. "Maybe I can let someone know where I am. I hope the emergency locator beacon is working. I've never trusted those beacons, but they've worked for others. I have some doubts about an electronic device that's supposed to begin working, by itself, after going through something as violent as an airplane crash."

"Man, it's quiet without the engine running. There isn't a breath of wind. No birds singing. No sound in this black-and-white place. Where am I? I don't know. Oh, wow, here we go again. I'm beginning to answer my own questions. Now I know I'm in trouble."

"How can I tell someone where I am if I don't know myself? Okay, I'm in a plane on a flight from Chicago to Minneapolis. Only I'm not flying anymore. How do I know this is northern Minnesota? Think. Come on, Brian, think it through. What happened?"

"Damn, now I'm beginning to remember some of it. I didn't refuel in Chicago. I must have really messed-up my fuel-on-board estimate. I should have refueled. There's no excuse for that kind of mistake," he chastised himself.

His mind created a vision of Len sitting at the table they used during his ground school sessions. *Brian, always remember to top up your fuel tanks before every flight out of your local area. There is absolutely no excuse for running low, or, what's worse, running out of gas during any flight.*

He looked around. In a voice now showing signs of weakness from cold and blood loss, he said, "Boy, did this flight turn into a disaster. That snowball really got big in a hurry. I think I'm somewhere around Alexandria. But, why do I think that? I should've gotten under the fog while I still had fuel enough to maneuver the plane. That's two bonehead mistakes I shouldn't have made. I know better than that."

Scotty realized he needed to find help. He reached for the microphone and turned on the power. He checked the frequency to see if he was on Alexandria flight service frequency, he was. He brought the microphone to his lips.

"Mayday, Mayday, this is Bonanza three two one one victor. Do you read?" Nothing. *The radio might not be working,* he thought. Slowly and carefully, he twisted the receiver dial till he found a navigation beacon. He identified it as the Alex beacon. "Well, the radio receiver is working," he said. He switched back to Alex flight service, and tried again.

"Mayday, Mayday, this is Bonanza three two one one victor. Do you read me?" He didn't hear a return call. He closed his eyes to rest. The disappointment was taking its toll. He fell into a fitful sleep. After a few minutes his eyes snapped open. He cried out, "Where the hell is everyone?"

Showing signs of panic, he began talking to the right seat as though someone were sitting there. "This is a busy area, there's bound to be an aircraft overhead sooner or later. Maybe they'll be on the Alex frequency and will relay a message. Now I guess we wait."

His eyes closed again and his chin dropped onto his chest. After a few minutes, his head lifted, his eyes opened and in a tired voice said, "I wonder if I reported my emergency status. If I did, they should be looking for us. That is, if the emergency locator beacon is working."

His whole body began shivering. He hugged himself with his one good arm. The trembling racked his body. He looked into the back seat and saw his topcoat on the floor. It appeared to be within reach.

As he turned his body, he caught his breath, and a whimper escaped his lips. He kept reaching until he caught a sleeve. He pulled the coat over the seat back and wrapped it around his shoulders and body as best he could.

After a few minutes, the trembling slowed. He talked to the right seat again. "Damn, it's cold—I'm bleeding again—hope someone hears us soon. We could bleed to death or freeze before anyone finds us. Need to get some pressure on the wound to stop the bleeding."

"I forgot about my survival kit. The first aid kit is on the back of the passenger seat. He reached into the back and ran his hand over the back of the passenger's seat. The first aid box wasn't in the holder. He strained to look on the floor. He couldn't see it and the pain of twisting his body was making his vision blur.

He waited until it cleared and noticed his seat belt was still fastened. He released the belt and looked for the first aid kit on the floor, both in the back seat and the front. At last he spotted it. The kit was just out of reach, down by the rudder pedals on the passenger's side.

He stretched as far as he could without causing his eyes to blur again. It remained about six inches beyond his reach and blood began seeping from his injuries again. He had to get that kit. Scotty looked around the cockpit for something he could use to coax the kit a little closer to him. Then he saw the cord that was attached to a ceiling panel. The other end of that cord had earphones attached.

He loosened the cord from the ceiling connector and pulled it toward him. The earphones caught on the edge of the passenger seat. He flipped the cord a few times and the earphones released the seat. Very carefully he tried to get the earphones to land behind the first aid kit but it was under the pedals. After five frustrating minutes he was able to get the box away from the pedals and within his reach.

Within a few minutes he had applied disinfectant and secured bandages on most of the bad wounds, with the exception of his left arm. He had tried to get out of his suit jacket, but the effort had totally drained his strength and the jacket continued to resist all of his efforts.

His eyes began drooping again. He snapped them open and shook his head. "Don't close your eyes. Stay awake. I think I'm going into shock. I can't afford that. Hang on. I've got to get us out of this mess.

"I should have listened. That crusty old lady, one of the smartest I've ever met. She knew what was coming. She tried to warn me. I knew better. I was smarter. Now I'm going to be dead if I can't raise help."

He picked up the microphone, got it somewhere close to his mouth, and in a weak voice said, "Mayday, Mayday, this is Bonanza one one victor. Does anyone read me?" He released the mic switch and listened. "Come on, answer, please." Nothing.

Fighting back tears and in a soft voice Scotty said, "Boy, is Mom going to give me hell. So will Grace. Oh, Grace, what have I done? If I die here, Billy will never know his dad. Lord, I'm so dumb. Please help me out of this jam. Don't let my son be without a father. I've always been mister safety, never leaving anything to chance, but, boy, did I foul up this time. I'm really sorry for this, Ben. At least it wasn't one of your airplanes. It was my pride and joy."

Chapter Four

B RIAN BEGAN WORKING FOR LEN ON SATURDAY MORNING. Len showed him the proper procedure for refueling an aircraft by showing him how to refuel his Piper Cherokee. He would be making a trip up into Michigan today. He taught him how to check the oil and check for contaminants in the fuel. That was something that needed to be done before every flight and was part of the pre-flight checklist on all aircraft.

Next Len took him into the hangar, showing him where to find brooms, mops, pails, and the cleaning supplies necessary to do that part of his job. He had the service hanger, two other storage hangers that belonged to the flight service, the customer lounge, front desk areas, and the flight line to keep clean.

"I want the service hanger cleaned and straightened up daily. Possibly you'll have to do it twice a day if we're doing a lot of service work. The other two hangers need sweeping once a day. The floors in those hangers need washing once a week or whenever they start looking dirty. All oil should be cleaned up as soon as it's spilled or seen by you. I don't ever want to see oil or grease on the floor of any of the hangers," Len said with a straight face.

"Clean the customer lounge whenever you think it needs it but at least once a day, twice a day on holidays and weekends. The flight line can be swept as needed with the tractor sweeper. Be sure you pick up any loose tie downs and wheel chocks. We don't want someone's prop-wash blowing those items into another plane and causing damage.

"Refueling a customer's aircraft will be one of your duties as soon as you learn how to handle some of the other aircraft types. For now Barbara, Buster, or I will handle the refueling chores. As time allows, I'll teach you how to handle the more popular aircraft. For now you can start by cleaning the customer's lounge and front desk area. Then do the service and storage hangers."

Brian picked up the cleaning supplies and began his career in aviation. For the next few hours he cleaned and polished the four buildings until they glistened. He got the keys to the sweeper and worked on the flight line until it was totally free of anything wind blown. In between, Len showed him how to refuel a high wing aircraft like a Cessna. He also learned about auxiliary fuel tanks and where most of them were located.

His first day on the job filled him with wonder and excitement about the future. He didn't want to quit when the day was over. Len had to tell him to go home. He would be back bright and early the next day. He climbed on his bike and slowly peddled back home. When he got there, Kim was waiting. "What happened? Did you learn how to fly?"

"No, I didn't learn how to fly. I probably won't learn that for at least another year, possibly more. But I learned a lot. I learned that a clean shop is required to work on airplanes. I learned how to refuel a plane. I learned safely and that airplanes must be handled very carefully. Oh, Kim, it was great. I can't wait to get back tomorrow."

For the rest of the summer, Brian worked hard every Wednesday through Sunday. Monday and Tuesday he spent watching the planes come and go. He soaked up knowledge about flying seven days a week. He did everything asked of him by Len and Barbara and still kept up with his family chores.

Brian spent his evenings reading books on how an aircraft was built, why they flew, why different aircraft designs were better at some things than others, and how the flight characteristics changed with weight and weather conditions. He went to the library and found books on servicing an aircraft in the field and in the shop.

His parents were beginning to worry about him, because he hadn't been out with his friends for many weeks. School would be starting soon and Brian hadn't had a vacation. At supper one evening in early August, Bill broached the subject of a family vacation. Brian's first question was, "How long will we be gone?"

Bill said, "We thinking about a one-week fishing trip. We thought the change of scenery and a little rest and relaxation would be good for you before school starts. Do you think you could spare a few days for your family?"

Brian smiled and said, "I guess I have been pretty busy this summer. I didn't mean to short change you guys, but this is very serious stuff. It's important to my future and to me. Fishing? You bet! I'd love to go fishing with you before school starts. I'll talk to Len tomorrow morning. When do you want to leave?"

"Next Saturday morning," Mae said.

"Count on it," Brian said. He excused himself and went up to his room to read about the flight characteristics of a Beechcraft V35 Bonanza. It was rapidly becoming one of his favorite planes.

The next morning, Brian asked to talk with Len before he had to leave on a charter to New York. He wouldn't get back until Monday night and he wanted to make sure he could go fishing with the family. Len was in the office doing paperwork for the charter when Brian walked in.

"Good morning Brian. You're here early this morning. Is there something you need or want to talk about?"

"Yes, there is. The family wants to go on a fishing vacation next Saturday. I wanted to find out if I could have the week off, so I could go with them," Brian said.

"Absolutely, you can. I think it's a fine idea. You've worked very hard this summer and learned a lot faster then I thought you would. We're ahead of schedule with ground school. I think a little rest and relaxation will do you a lot of good. Besides, I'm going to start you working in the service shop with Buster soon. You need to get some hands-on experience with engines and airframes. Maybe we'll do that when you come back. By that time I'll have some more books you'll need to read.

"But, while you're on vacation, I want you to leave all your study materials home. Take something to read for pleasure if you want, but no books on flying" Len said smiling at Brian.

A smile raced across Brian's face when he heard Len's words. "Thanks, Len." He whirled about and started for the door, slamming to a stop just before he cleared the room, "Have a safe flight," he said. Then he was gone.

Brian was sweeping the ramp when Len came out of the office and waved him over to the hanger. When he got there, Len had the tow bar attached to the nose wheel of the Cessna 310. Brian backed the tractor up to hook the tow bar to the hitch. When it snapped into place, he slowly towed the Cessna out to the flight line, jumped off the tractor and put the wheel chocks in place.

He quickly disconnected the tow bar and returned it to the hanger. By the time Len came out of the office, Brian had the ramp swept clean. Len waved his thanks to Brian, loaded his passengers into the Cessna, fired up the engines, and taxied to the active runway.

One minute after Len cleared the runway, a student pilot, landed a Piper 140 hard and blew a tire. The student pilot lost control of the plane and the instructor didn't, or couldn't, move fast enough to make the necessary corrections. The plane ground looped on the runway and ended up in the grass strip between the runway and the taxi strip.

Brain saw the whole thing and was running to the office before the ground loop started. He burst through the door shouting to Barbara, "A plane just blew a tire and ground looped into the grass. It looks damaged but no fire, yet."

He ran out with the fire bottle from the office and jumped on the tractor. He raced as fast as the tractor would go and arrived at the plane the same time the student and his instructor climbed out. With fire bottle in hand, he jumped down from the tractor and ran to the plane. Still no fire and both occupants looked okay.

The fire department arrived a few minutes later, looked at the plane, and turned around and left. The plane suffered a bent prop, scraped nose cowl, and the right wing tip had been crumpled. Not major damage, but enough to keep the plane on the ground until repairs could be made.

Buster had heard the commotion and had loaded a trailer with a tow bar, hand tools, a wing jack, and a landing gear cradle: a device that attached to the landing gear, allowing the plane be towed using the cradle's wheels.

Brian hooked up the trailer. With Buster sitting on the back of the trailer, they drove back out to the crash site. Brian attached the tow bar while Buster looked at the damage. With coaching from Buster, Brian carefully towed the plane back onto the runway. Buster positioned the jack and got the plane high enough to attach the cradle. With Buster at the tractor controls and Brian walking close to the wing tip on the damaged side, they made their way back to the hanger.

Buster positioned the Piper in the back corner. He knew it would take a few days for the FAA and the insurance company to come around to inspect the damage, and he didn't want the Piper in his way. In this shop, Buster was king and what he said was the law.

Brian felt great when Buster turned to him, after everything had settled down and all the tools and equipment had been returned to its rightful place, and said, "Good job, kid. You did everything just like the book says it should be done. I like that." Then he went back to work and Brian began cleaning the hanger.

Saturday morning, Brian was up early and helped his dad load the car. By the time they finished, breakfast was ready. After breakfast, Kim and Brian washed the dishes. Mae straightened up the house and fussed over being rushed into the car. Two hours later they unloaded everything into the three-bedroom cabin that would be their home for the next week.

Brian and his father spent a lot of time in the boat, talking about Brian's future in aviation. Bill still wasn't sold on the course Brian had selected. He advised, "I feel that aviation isn't a good career for you, son. I believe you should seriously think about becoming a lawyer, doctor, or go into the retail business. At the very least, something more legitimate than being a pilot or an airplane mechanic. And, you know how your mother feels about the airline business."

Bill tried his best, but Brian just wouldn't be swayed. For every argument Bill brought up, Brian had a positive reason why it wouldn't work or wasn't right for him. Finally, Bill realized he had no chance of changing his son's mind and lapsed into silence and serious fishing.

Brian was getting fidgety by Friday morning. He was out of bed and dressed by 6:00. He walked out on the dock and sat down on the bench. He watched the gentle waves coming in from the northwest, his mind racing. All he could think about was starting in the shop with Buster. He was really looking forward to it. He wondered if Buster would start with engines or with airframes. He hoped it would be engines. Airframes were just not as exciting as engines.

Kim joined him on the bench an hour later. They talked about school and Kim's almost boyfriend, Jack Stubbelfield. They laughed again about Brian's intimating Italian uncles in Chicago being gangsters. Kim had gone out with Jack since that conversation, but he hadn't tried to get her into the back seat for any heavy necking.

"I really like Jack, but I'm not ready for that part of the relationship yet. Maybe in a few years, but not now," she confided.

"Let's not have the both of us give the folks a bad time. I'm giving them fits with airplanes and flying. Play it straight with Jack, but tell him how you feel. Don't do anything you'll be sorry for later," he advised.

"Mom and Dad are really worried about you, Brian. They think you've taken on too much. They won't ask you to give up your dream but they sure wish you would."

"I know, Kim, but aviation has taken hold of my gut and it just won't let go. I've got to keep going as long as I can."

About that time Mae opened the door and called "Brian, Kim, breakfast is ready."

"Let's eat," Brian said. "Thanks for caring, Kim."

"That's okay, big brother."

All too soon it was Saturday again and Brian had a serious case of mixed emotions. He wanted to prolong the vacation and time with his family, but also he wanted to get on with his passion. But now, it was time to go home.

Brian helped his father pack the car while Mae and Kim cleaned and straightened the cabin. None of them wanted to leave, but their vacation was over. School would be starting bright and early Monday morning. *It'll be an exciting year,* Brian thought.

It was an exciting year. During that year, Brian worked at the airport after school and on the weekends. He continued to read everything he could find in the library and the books that Len gave him. His ground school went well and his report cards continued to be all A's. He completed a term paper in his English class on the life and times of, "The Wright Brothers during the period of development of the Wright Flyer." That earned him an A+ in his English class. The only downer was that Len put off starting him working with Buster.

His studies with Len were now well ahead of schedule. Brian was a quick study and very accurate in his answers to Len's oral quizzes. So Len took him well beyond what was needed to pass his written test for a student license. By the end of the school year, Brian was at the top of his class and still going strong.

Chapter Five

B RIAN MET KIM AFTER SCHOOL and they compared class schedules. Brian, as a Junior, had what he thought was the tougher schedule. Kim didn't agree.

"Kim, my first three classes are bearcats. Look at them. English first period, Math second period, and Physics just before lunch. Boy, that's a tough morning."

"I see that, but look at your afternoon. All you have are Machine shop, a study hall, and Physical Ed. That's a breeze," she commented. "Now, mine is a heavy schedule of homework classes."

This good-natured bantering lasted all the way home with Brian lugging all of his own books and most of Kim's. They trudged up the stairs and separated into their own rooms to begin the task of homework for yet another year.

On top of his school homework, Brian had ground school books he needed to study in order to pass the test for his student flying permit. Len had started him with what he thought was the single most important factor in flying safely, beyond the aircraft itself, of course: Weather. He also taught him how to read weather maps, understand weather movement, and above all, to expect the unexpected in weather development. This was followed very closely by dead reckoning navigation and then radio navigation.

Brian's evenings and weekends were dedicated to school and flying, but he didn't mind. Soon, he would be in the air piloting an airplane. *I could do it all. I will do it all with the help of Len and my family I will become a good pilot. No, a great pilot,* he thought.

By Christmas break Brian was beginning to show a little strain. His report card still showed all A's and he was able to answer all the oral quizzes Len gave him, but he was having trouble getting up early every morning even though he went to bed early. Bill and Mae could see the changes in Brian. She talked it over with Bill, and they decided they had to let Brian make his own decisions.

Brian saw that his classes in the second half of the school year would be just as tough. In fact they could be a little tougher because a history class would replace machine shop. That would mean more homework. He thought about it all evening and by bedtime he had made a decision. He would talk to Len when he went into work the next morning.

Len was in his office when Brian arrived. He went to the door and asked, "Len, can I talk with you a minute?"

"Sure, Brian, come in and sit down. What's the good word? I hear your grades stayed up and your studies here are still ahead of schedule."

Brian hesitated for a moment and said, "Len I would like to take the holidays off. I'm tired and getting a little stale. Yes, my grades stayed all A's, but my English class was a little shaky. I'd like some time to work on it and to rest a little."

"It's a great idea," Len responded. "Take as much time as you need. As I said, your ground school is ahead of schedule. You're just about ready to take your written test and I want you sharp for that. All you have left is to get Federal Aviation Regulations down. Besides, I have a couple tests I want to give you before you take the written test for your license and we need to discuss pre-flight safety issues, again. Why don't you start that rest today? I'll see you the Saturday after school starts again."

"Thanks, Len, I think I will," Brian answered.

For the next six days, he visited with friends, read what he wanted to read, cleaned his room, and helped his mother and dad with chores around the house. After the fourth day he realized something was missing. By the sixth day he realized what it was—he wasn't learning anything about flying airplanes. After the supper dishes were finished, he went to his room and closed the door.

Christmas Day dawned bright and crisply cold. The MacTavish family went to early church services together. Brian and Kim were strangely quiet all morning. This just wasn't the way the MacTavish children acted Christmas.

After returning from church, Mae retired to the kitchen, bringing out pots and pans and gathering the raw materials to create the family favorites. This year it was going to be turkey, mom's real mashed potatoes, green bean casserole, and mincemeat pie. Mae had tried the new instant mashed potatoes when they had first come into the market. She didn't like them. It just wasn't the same as real homemade mashed potatoes.

As she was contemplating where to start, Brian walked into the kitchen. "Mom, can I help you with something?"

Mae was startled. "You don't have to help me," she replied, "but you can if you want. Start by peeling the potatoes." She paused, "Is there something wrong, Brian?"

"No Mom, I'm fine. I guess I'm just a little bored or suffering from a lack of something to study. I'm so used to hitting the books every evening that I'm lost with nothing to study. I'll admit I needed the rest but now I'm ready to go again."

"Where are you going now?" Kim asked as she walked into the kitchen.

"I'm not going anywhere," Brian answered. "Mom and I were talking about what I'm studying and how much I needed this time to rest. What you overheard was me telling Mom that I'm getting bored with nothing to study and I'm ready to go again."

"I don't know how you can keep all your school work and this flying thing separated enough to learn anything," Kim commented. "What does Len have you working on now?"

"Len says we're ahead of schedule with ground school. I need to finish that and then I'll be able to take the written test for my student pilot's license. Once that's in my pocket, I can start flying. Len says that after I've had twenty or twenty-five hours of duel instruction, I should be ready to solo. That's flying the plane alone. The only part of ground school I'm not comfortable with is navigation. Doing wind triangles, plotting the course, computing fuel consumption, estimated flight time, and then filing flight plans on paper is fine, but I'm having trouble understanding how it all comes together in the cockpit. Kim nodded as Brian continued.

"All of that paperwork needs to be done before you even consider getting in the plane. You need a list of frequencies of all the electronic navigational aids along your route, maps, and any hazards or notams—those are notices to airman that might give you trouble along the way.

"Then, you have to know where you are at all times, either by visual contact with the ground or radio navigation. That way you can tell if you're still on course and where you should be along that course. It all has to match what's on your flight plan. I don't know how I'll be able to do all those things and still fly the plane at the same time. Maybe after I do a couple of flights it'll sink in."

Kim continued to press for information, "When does he think you will be ready to take the test?"

"He thinks in a month or so I'll be ready."

Mae put her arms around her son. "You just take the time you need. As long as you insist on pursuing this flying career I want you to do everything right and safe. I would rather you take a little longer to accomplish your dream then rushing through it. I know you'll accomplish it. I just don't want you to hurt yourself in the process."

"I won't hurt myself, Mom. I promise."

CHAPTER SIX

SCOTTY'S EYES OPENED SLOWLY. He had been reliving the flight to Chicago in that old Ford Tri-plane. He glanced around the cockpit and realized his current situation. It came slamming back at him.

He checked his wounds for bleeding. All had stopped except for his left arm, but that appeared to be nothing more than a little seepage. He was still cold. He pulled the wool coat a little closer to his body. He looked out at the clearing again. It was dark now.

How am I going to get help? I tried the radio and I couldn't raise the tower. That says I'm too far away from the airfield for them to hear my transmissions from the ground. Maybe the antenna has been torn off. No, that's not it. I can see it right in front of me on the cowl. I can receive the navigation beacon but I can't reach the control tower. His mind began working on the options. He needed help, and soon!

As long as the weather is still marginal there won't be any traffic into the airfield. He remembered the flare pistol he had added to his emergency survival kit. Unfortunately that was in the baggage area along with his winter clothes and tools. *The radio still seems to be my only way of communicating with the outside world,* he thought.

The pains in his whole body were beginning to get worse. His legs were now becoming painful but not overly so. Feeling was returning to both of his legs. They were painful at the moment and he could feel the cold seeping into his toes. He thought again about trying to get out of the plane to build a fire to keep warm. *There might be a little fuel left in the auxillary tank behind the seat. I can use that to start a fire.* He thought.

No, I'd probably set fire to myself because I can't move fast enough to get out of the way or I might spill some of the fuel on me. That would be the final disaster. I'm trying to save my life not end it.

He found his map case on the floor behind his seat. He carefully pulled it over the passenger seat and set it down. He opened it and found what he wanted, a bottle of fresh water. He slipped the bottle under his right leg and twisted the cap until it was loose. He removed the cap and took a mouthful. Slowly, he let it trickle down his throat.

"Oooh, that's good." He replaced the screw cap and set it upright on the seat next to the map case. "Now back to the problems at hand."

Scotty was becoming very tired. His eyes were burning and he wanted to close them and sleep. "No! Keep your eyes open dummy and keep your mind working on the problems. I can't afford to sleep yet. Not until I can be assured of help coming. And, we ain't there yet."

He let his mind open to other things. All of a sudden he opened his map case again and began rummaging around inside. "I know it's here somewhere. Grace told me she had put it in my case, just in case it got cold. She said it would go well with my new coat." He pulled out all the sectional maps and through them on the floor.

A smile cracked his face and he pulled a long, bright red scarf from the bottom of the case. "Maybe I can find a way to get this on the radio antenna. With all the white around me it would stand out." He opened the small-hinged window and tried to reach the antenna rod only inches away from the windshield. He couldn't reach it using his right arm. It just didn't bend the right way and his left arm was useless.

He closed his eyes and let his mind settle down allowing his breathing to return back to normal. He opened his eyes and looked around for a way to get the scarf outside so it could be seen. Once again his eyes focused on the earphones attached to the long wire cord.

"Maybe I can flip the earphones with the scarf tied to them up on the roof of the cabin. It's pretty flat up there and the earphones are heavy. There isn't any wind so it shouldn't blow off. It would make the white top of the plane a little easier to see. Let's give it a try."

He wedged the connector end of the cable into a crevasse in the seat to keep him from losing the whole thing. It took him six tries but he finally got it onto the roof. He gave it a tentative tug and it didn't move. It must have caught something on the roof that would keep it up there.

Now he really was tired, he was getting a queasy stomach too. The pain in his left arm was getting very bad and his legs were causing him some worry. They were getting very cold even with the wool coat covering most of them. "It's going to be a long night and I'm cold already."

Scotty thought about the time he began working with Buster in the shop. How proud he was to be working with Buster. He could see it all again: *"Come over here, kid," he ordered.* "First, if you're going to work with me, you gotta have a nick name. So, from now on, at least in this hanger, you're Scotty. When I call your name, you come a runnin'. When I give you something to do, you do it. When I'm teachin', you listen. If you have a question, you ask. Do you agree with these ground rules?"

"Yes, sir," Scotty answered.

"No, not sir. I'm Buster. You remember that too. Now, let's get to work. We got the go-ahead from the insurance company to start the repairs on that Piper that ground looped. You can help me get it up on jacks and then you can drain all the fluids out of her."

Buster showed him where the jacks were to be placed and explained how the procedure would work. They raised the plane high enough to allow a comfortable working position under the wing. Then, he showed him how to drain the fuel tanks and engine oil sump. When he had finished, he said, "Okay, Scotty, it's all yours. When you get the fluids drained and properly disposed of, come and get me."

For the rest of the day, Scotty carefully performed the tasks Buster assigned him. The time flew by, and before he realized it, it was time to quit.

Buster called Scotty, "Come over to the bench." Scotty dropped what he was doing and ran to where Buster was standing.

"I got a bunch of books for you to study. The first thing we'll do is get you ready for your airframe license test. I want you to study these first two books. At the end of each chapter is a short test. On a separate sheet of paper, I want you to write the answers to the questions and bring it in to me. When you have time, do the first three chapters."

"School's out for the summer, so I can start these books right away. I should be able to get them done in a couple of days."

"That's great, but don't rush it," Buster said. And shaking his finger in front of Scotty's face he added, "Just make sure you understand everything you read, and by all means, ask questions about anything you don't understand. Now get out of here. I'll see you tomorrow morning."

In two weeks, Scotty had finished both books. He had taken all the end-of-chapter tests and hadn't missed a question. The Piper 140 was coming along quickly with both of them working on it. The undercarriage had been repaired and they were working on the sheet metal damage.

THE CLEARING WAS BEGINNING to return to normal. He had heard the songs of Minnesota's Timber Wolves earlier in the evening and some of the night birds had flown in to check out this strange looking bird that lay in their territory. A great horned owl had settled down on what was left of the engine cowling.

His thoughts drifted into a mist and for the moment he couldn't think of anything. His mind had shut down. He let his eyes close and his chin dropped to his chest.

As these thoughts brought back pleasant memories, Scotty came back to reality. Dawn was lightening up the horizon. Unfortunately the fog was still present all the way to the ground.

CHAPTER SEVEN

BY MID-JANUARY BRIAN WAS BACK IN FULL STRIDE. His classes were back to where he had confidence in his grade average with the exception of his new History class. He might need to ask Kim for some help. He had worked hard on navigation and he felt he had a good handle on that, but this history thing was giving him fits.

Len had given him a written test on weather forecasting. He passed the test with a perfect score. Over the next six weeks, when Len wasn't on a charter, he and Brian spent several hours together in the office, out on the flight line, or in the hanger. Len wanted him letter perfect on pre-flight safety checks, how to read weather briefings, how to file flight plans, and of the most important parts, navigation. Len showed him where to find notices to airman, (NOTAMs) and how to interpret them.

Len was impressed with Brian's ability to grasp an idea and work his way through it to a logical conclusion. He was a quick study and he retained what he learned. By the first part of April Len had started Brian studying Federal Aviation Regulations and throwing verbal questions at him when he least expected it. By the end of the month, Len pronounced him ready to take the student license test.

He talked to the local FAA test center, and set an appointment at 8:00 on Saturday morning May twenty-third. He found Brian in the service hanger, sweeping the floor. He walked up to him with a very serious expression on his face. "Brian, I need to talk with you a moment."

When he finished, Brian's mouth was open and he had a shocked look on his face. Slowly he closed his mouth, his lips turned up at the corners and a smile swept rapidly across his face. "Oh, wow! That's great news. That gives me a couple of weeks to prepare. This is great. I can hardly wait. Thanks a lot, Len," he stammered.

"Two days before the test, I want you to close the books and just think of something else. I want you to answer the questions as quickly and honestly as you can. Trust your knowledge and yourself," Len said. With that, he walked across the hanger and into his office.

Brian studied up to that Wednesday night, then, closed the books. He was full of confidence. Saturday morning came and so did the jitters. Brian rose early. By 6:00 he had finished breakfast and was pacing the floor. At 7:00 he mounted his bike and started for the FAA test facility.

As he rode out of the yard, Kim leaned out of her second-floor bedroom window and shouted, "Good luck, Brian."

He waved his thanks back at her and peddled down the road. At ten minutes to eight he walked in the door of the testing facility and checked in at the desk. The woman behind the desk handed him some papers to fill out and pointed to a table a few feet away. He quickly filled in the requested information and returned the papers to the woman. She handed him the test booklet and answer sheet and said, "You can start the test now."

Twenty minutes later he handed the answer sheet and the test booklet back to the woman. "We will notify you, by letter, in a few weeks. If you pass, the confirmation will have a student license enclosed," she said. She saw a nervous twitch and a downcast look on Brian's face. She added, "We aren't busy this morning. I'll tell you what. I'll grade the paper now, but only as far as seventy-percent correct. That's all that's necessary to get the license. At least you'll know if you made it."

"Thank you, that would be great," Brian said.

In a few minutes, she looked up from her work and commented, "Well, Mister MacTavish, you've passed your test. When the FAA sends your student license, they'll give you your test score on the confirmation."

A beaming Brian, quietly, thanked the woman for her help and walked out the door. He straddled his bike and whispered, "I'm on my way."

Brian went back to the airport and told Len about the test and what a nice person the lady was. He told Len she had graded the test for him until she had reached the seventy-percent score needed for passage.

Len said, "Now I suppose you want to start flying. Well, we'll talk about that when I see the license and the score you achieved. For now, clean up the flight line. There's sand on the ramp around the fueling area."

As Brian went out the door he thought, *maybe Len would start my flight training, now.* He had passed his ground school with a perfect score, he had passed his student pilots license test without a mistake to the seventy-percent score, and now he was ready to fly.

Two weeks later the license arrived in the mail. Along with the license came a letter of congratulations from the department head. The letter told him he had passed the test with a perfect score. He rushed to the airport and showed the letter to Len. He could hardly talk. "Now, can we start my duel instruction?"

"Okay, now we can start. How about tomorrow morning? Be here at eight o'clock. But remember, only one hour of duel at a time. Now I want you to take the day off. Go home and study your preflight procedures and FARs."

"Thanks, Len. See you in the morning."

When Brian had left the airport grounds, Len walked over to the service hanger and talked to Buster. "I want you to drain a quart of oil out of the Cessna 150 trainer. Loosen the hinge on the left aileron. Brian is starting his first lesson tomorrow morning. I want to see if he's paying attention to safety issues even when he's excited."

"Good plan. If you don't have a requirement the rest of the day, I'll do it now."

"No, I just checked the book and no one wants to check it out. Be sure you mark it as grounded, though. I'd hate to have someone else rent it out," Len commented.

Brian showed up at exactly eight o'clock Sunday morning. Len told him to roll out the Cessna trainer and preflight it. He would be right out. Brian walked across the flight line to the hanger and hooked the tow bar to the Cessna and pulled the plane out. He returned the tow bar and tug to the hanger, and started the preflight inspection.

The first thing he checked was the oil. Without saying a word to anyone, he added the missing quart of oil. He checked the engine compartment for bird nests or other foreign objects, and then he began his walk-around inspection of the airplane. He checked the tires for cuts and air pressure, he checked wing struts for tightness and damage, and he systematically checked all of the control surfaces.

He found the left aileron outboard hinge had several loose screws. That wasn't right, because they were attached with lock nuts and safety wire. He went back into the hanger and told Buster what he had found. "Buster, that isn't right. Maybe the safety wire has broken and let the screw back out a little. It isn't real loose but it isn't right. I think we need to check it out before we take it up."

"Roll the bird back in the hanger. I'll take a look at it. You go and tell Len what you found," Buster ordered.

Brian did as he was told. Later, Buster came into Len's office and reported, "Brian was right, the safety wire had broken. I tightened the hinge and put on new safety wire."

"Good job Brian. Did you finish the preflight?" Len asked.

"Yes, I did. I added a quart of oil but I haven't recorded it in the book yet."

"Take care of the paper work and roll it back out and we'll go flying."

When Brian had left the office, Len looked at Buster and commented, "It looks like we have a good one on our hands. By the way, I'm going to have Brian working with you all the time this summer."

"I'll be glad to help him. I'll begin pulling books and things together. I could use the help this summer. We have several one-hundred-hour inspections coming up on our own planes, plus that banged up ground looper Brian and I have already started. That will give him a good foundation to get his mechanics license," Buster said.

For the next hour, Brian was in heaven. For the first time in his life, he had the controls of an aircraft in his hands with the engine running. He was giddy with excitement on the inside. On the outside he was all business.

Len instructed Brian, "Check weather from the flight service station and then set the altimeter to the barometer setting they give you."

After receiving the weather briefing and setting the altimeter, Len explained, "In this airplane you steer it using the rudder pedals. Now I want you to contact ground control and ask permission to taxi to the active runway. When you get permission, follow the instructions they give you and proceed to the end of the active runway." When they arrived, Brian took out the preflight checklist, without being told, and performed each task very carefully.

When they were both satisfied that all was well, Len said, "I'll do the first takeoff. I want you to keep your hands and feet on the controls and follow what I do. Pick up the microphone and ask the tower for takeoff clearance."

When they received clearance, Len advanced the throttle, turned into the middle of the runway and started the takeoff. *Flight training has finally started*, Brian thought.

That first takeoff was thrilling. So much so, that it just about brought tears to his eyes. He kept his hands lightly on the control yoke and his feet on the rudder-peddles, following every move Len made. As soon as they had left the airport control area, Len told him to take the controls, and he coached him through his first turns. Brian was all business but a little nervous and his movements were tentative.

Before he realized it, the hour was over and they were returning to the airport. Len instructed him on the proper procedure to receive permission to enter the traffic pattern and how to fly a good pattern and approach for landing. Len then took the controls back and told him to keep his hands and feet on the controls and follow his movements through the landing.

Len called ground control and received permission to taxi to his ramp. "Okay, Brian you get us back to the hanger and park the plane next to the gas pump. I want you to refuel it and then move the plane back into the hanger."

Brian's stomach was shaking but his hands and feet were rock solid and he handled the controls like they were glass. When he had the plane parked next to the fuel pump, he set the parking brake, and shut off the fuel supply to the engine. He sat there for a moment and then released his seat belt and opened the door.

Len had exited the plane as soon as Brian had shut down the engine and walked into the office. Brian couldn't think straight yet. His mind was still in the sky flying this little trainer. Slowly he came back to earth and began refueling the plane. When he had the trainer back in the hanger, he walked into the office, and Len called him in to talk.

Len asked him to sit down and held out a little book to him. "Here's your first flight log book. For now, I'll make all of the entries in it. When you solo, you will make all the entries. Every time you fly, you need to record everything you did and the type of plane you were flying. Keep it with you in a briefcase because somewhere along the line, an official will ask to see it. If you rent a plane from another flight service, they'll want to know the type of aircraft you are familiar with, Brian nodded.

"For now, I want you to think about what we did today. Next lesson I want you to show me that you learned something today. Now go home and enjoy the feeling of what you started. We'll do it again Saturday morning."

Brian left the airport on his bike. He was thrilled. He had flown an airplane today. He couldn't quite get a grip on his thoughts, but he knew this is what he was meant to do.

On the last day of school, Brian got his report card. Once again it was straight "A's" except in History. That was a "B-." That was too close so he decided to ask Kim to give him some coaching. Kim asked to see his report card during the bus ride home. She just shook her head and mumbled under her breath, "Genius. But what happened to History?"

That evening at the dinner table, Bill asked Brian, "Well, let's see your grades."

"Gee, Dad, I'm sorry. I forgot all about it." He got up from the table, went into his bedroom, and returned with the report card. "Here it is. I think you'll be happy with what you see."

Bill looked at it, passed it over to Mae, and looked at Brian. A big smile cracked his face and in an off-hand manner, commented, "Good job, son but what happened to History?"

Brian got a sheepish look on his face and answered, "I did have some problems, but I'll bring it up before the next report card."

On Monday morning Brian got up early, fixed his own breakfast, washed his dishes, and was ready to leave for the airport when his mother came downstairs. He gave her a kiss on the cheek, told her he had fixed his own breakfast, and he would see her for supper.

"Just a moment, young man," she said. "What about lunch?"

"I'll pick up a sandwich at the airport," he answered. He bounded out the door and charged across the yard with bike pedals flying. He parked his bike at the side door of the service hanger and sauntered into the shop. Buster was already there, standing alongside a workbench in the back corner of the shop.

Buster called him over and told him they had permission to finish the repairs on the Piper ground looper. For the rest of the day Scotty did everything Buster told him had to be done. They worked together, and Scotty was in second heaven. He was learning from a master.

After Scotty had left for the day, Buster told Len that Scotty was a natural mechanic. "He does what I ask him to do, understands what he's doing, and why he's doing it. He handles tools well, and is very careful in his work. It's a pleasure to have him working beside me," Buster commented.

"For a crusty old loner like you, Buster, that's a big compliment," Len said.

Seven weeks after that first lesson, Len thought Scotty was ready to solo. He had twenty-two hours before this session started and he seemed to be doing very well. Len had him do a couple of stalls with controlled recovery and then two tail spins from high altitude. He asked him to let the plane spin once and then recover. Then he told him to do another, but this time let it turn one and a half times before recovery. Both spins were handled very well.

"Take us back to the field and land, Scotty."

When they reached the ramp, Scotty pulled up in front of the fuel pump and began the shutdown procedure when Len stopped him. "It's time, Scotty. I want you to take the plane back up by yourself. I want you to fly away about fifteen minuets west then return. I want to see two touch-and-go landings and then a final landing and return here. You got all that?"

Scotty had a grin a mile wide as he watched Len. "Solo time I guess. Yes, I think I can do everything you asked."

"Good luck, son. I know you can do it, I just need to see it done."

Scotty did as he was told and on his return, he called the tower and got his permission to do his two touch-and-go landings. "As he was on short final, no less than a mile from his first solo landing, another plane cut in front of him and lined up for a landing. Len, watching from the ramp, was shocked to see what this pilot had done. He heard the tower call out to the intruder to clear the area but he didn't respond or attempt to clear the runway.

Scotty saw what was happening, heard the tower's orders to the other plane and as calm as could be, he added power to his engine and slowly retracted the flaps and executed a perfect missed approach. He notified the tower of his actions and the tower thanked him for his quick thinking. He finished his touch-and-go requirement and his final landing.

As he taxied up to the hanger, he noted the other plane's pilot was being escorted back to the tower complex. Len met him as he pulled up to the pump. He shut down the engine and pulled the key from the ignition. Len opened the door, smiled and said, "Get out, young man. You have just passed your solo test in a rather unusual way. Great job! Here's your log book. It's now your responsibility. Did you get nervous on that first approach?"

"No, I wasn't. I was shocked to see something like that happen, but we've practiced missed approaches so it wasn't scary."

When they got back to the office, Barbara gave Scotty a big hug and then pulled his shirt back out of his pants and proceeded to cut a section of shirt tail off while everyone, including Buster laughed. Len walked over to the desk and said, "We'll start your cross-country training tomorrow."

By the end of summer, Scotty had his cross-country requirement finished. That fall, after school started, he worked at the airport only on weekends. He would stop at the airport after school to bring his test answers or questions to Buster. On Saturday, he would work with Buster in the shop and on Sundays, he would work on the ramp.

As time allowed, he practiced his piloting skills by shooting touch-and-go landings in all types of wind conditions and doing short cross-country trips using only contact, or dead reckoning, navigation. Scotty's grades continued to stay high with a lot of help from Kim in History.

Len was proud of his prize student. He told Mae and Bill that Scotty was becoming a fine pilot. What he didn't tell them was that he was afraid Scotty would become too cocky and lose sight of the safety part of flying. He soon found out he didn't have to worry. Len, Buster, and Barbara watched him very closely, and he never took short cuts or chances while working or flying.

One day, the following summer, Buster announced that Scotty would be ready to take his test for his airframe license. Len asked, "Are you sure? It's been only a year that you've been working with him. I don't want him to fail at this stage of his training."

"Listen, Len, that kid's a natural. He's learned more in that year than I learned in two years at aircraft school. He's a quick study and it stays with him. I don't have to remind him or tell him how to do something anymore. I just tell him what needs to be done and he does it, the right way. Yes, he's ready."

The next day, Len called Scotty into his office. "Buster tells me he believes you're ready to take the test for your airframe license. How do you feel about that?"

"Buster's a great teacher. If he thinks I'm ready, then I'm comfortable with that. From what Buster has told me about the test I know I can pass it."

"Okay, Scotty, I'll set up an appointment for you."

Three weeks later, Scotty took the test at the local FAA testing facility. Two weeks after that, he received his license in the mail. When he opened the envelope he screamed, "Yes!" He laughed like a crazy person and raced out of the house and down the road to the airport. He burst into the shop and raced over to Buster, laughing and hollering, "I got it! I got it!"

Buster watched him running across the hanger, shook his head, and turned back to his work. Scotty stopped dead in his tracks and looked confused. "Buster, I passed the test. I've got the license in my hands. Aren't you just a little happy for me?"

He looked over his shoulder at Scotty. "I taught you. When I say you're ready for the test, it's because you are. I didn't have any doubt in my mind that you'd pass. Go into my office. There's a frame on my desk. Put your license in it and hang it on the wall next to mine. Then come out here and help me finish this old Cessna." Scotty smiled and did as he was told.

Through the summer, Scotty worked with Buster, studied textbooks on aircraft engines, and during his free time, flew one of the training planes.

On the return leg of one of his cross-country flights, the Cessna 150 he was flying had a radio failure. There was only one radio in the plane. That meant he didn't have electronic navigation aids or communications with the ground, but that didn't give him a problem. He continued on his previous heading and switched to contact navigation.

When he reached the airport, he flew a triangle pattern just off the approach pattern. This maneuver informed the tower that a pilot had a communications problem. He continued this triangle until the tower saw him and flashed a green light—his second triangle. He then entered the traffic pattern and completed his landing.

When he got back to the office, he had the plane's log book in his hand. He sat down and wrote the problem into the log book then went to the blackboard where the entire rental aircraft were listed by number and wrote grounded behind the Cessna's number.

At that moment, Len came into the office and looked at what Scotty had written and asked, "What's the problem with the Cessna, Scotty?"

"I took it on a short cross country this afternoon and I lost the radio about half way back."

"Did you have any problem finding the airport or getting permission to land?" Len asked.

"No I didn't. I flew straight here by contact and flew a triangle just like you told me to. The tower flashed the green light at me and I made my landing. I've already made the log book entry but I thought I'd better ground the plane before someone else wanted to fly it."

"Good job," Len commented and walked out of the office.

He walked across the hanger toward Buster. As he approached him, Buster saw the look on his face and said, "What's the problem, Len?"

"No problem, but the radio's out on the Cessna trainer. It failed on Scotty during a cross-country flight. Scotty told me he didn't have a problem getting permission to land because he flew the triangle pattern just as I told him to and they gave him the green light. My problem with that explanation is, I haven't told him about emergency light signals yet." Len answered. He turned around and walked back toward his office, and Buster started chuckling to himself.

Summer vacation was coming to an end with Scotty building a lot of pilot-in-command hours in his log book and working with Buster on whatever came into the shop. He studied the textbooks that Buster gave him and when anything came into the shop regarding engines, Buster let Scotty work on it with him.

This was Scotty's senior year. Just one more year and he would be ready for college. He already knew what he wanted. He just didn't know what part of the business he wanted to study. He would think about that.

Scotty asked for Labor Day week off so he could rest before starting his last year of high school. The whole family took that time to vacation at a good fishing lake. By the first Monday after Labor Day, Scotty was ready for school.

CHAPTER EIGHT

SCOTTY AND KIM RODE THE BUS HOME FROM SCHOOL that first Monday. Kim was complaining about the amount of homework she had. Scotty laughed at her and said, "Kim, the classes you are taking are easy. I got A's in all of them."

"That's another point. These teachers are expecting me to be as bright as my genius big brother. There's no way I can compete with you." Kim said.

"This is my last year in this school. By this time next year they won't even remember my name. I'll help you with your homework, as you helped me, whenever and however I can," Scotty responded.

For the balance of the school year Scotty worked at the airport, flew when he had the time, and kept his grades where he wanted them. Thanks to a lot of help from sister, his life had turned into a safe monotony. By the time he graduated from high school at the top of his class, he had his private pilot's license and was well on his way to his commercial and instrument endorsements. By the end of the summer he had them both and had completed his duel instruction for multi-engine endorsement. His job classification at Boerger flight service had changed to pilot mechanic. Within two weeks, he had taken the flight test for multi-engine and passed without a problem.

Scotty enrolled at the University of Minnesota in the fall and started a very ambitious program in Aeronautical Engineering. In the first three years he had maintained a grade point average of 3.8 out of a possible 4.0, and had enough credits to get his degree after the first quarter of his fourth year, if he maintained his average. He went into the dean's office and asked if he could do the balance of his work by mail, because he wanted to pursue an out-of-town flying position. The dean said he would review his record and talk to his instructors.

Three days later, he called Scotty into his office and told him the engineering school would let him graduate at the end of the quarter if he satisfactorily completed a final paper on a related subject of his choice. Scotty agreed with a big smile, thanked the dean and walked out of the office.

Scotty hadn't told the dean his paper was already written. He had been working on it for the past three weeks. He was confident it was a good one. When he got home, he called Aircraft Unlimited in Chicago to set up an interview. He had sent them his resume two weeks earlier in response to a help wanted add in the paper. They called and requested an interview in Chicago. The following week he was sitting in the pilots' lounge at Gillette flying service talking with Mr. Ben Rosenberg, the owner of Aircraft Unlimited.

Mr. Rosenberg reviewed his school transcript, pilot's log book, letters of recommendation from instructors, and one letter from his friend and fellow pilot, Len Boerger. They talked for close to thirty minutes. Then, they both stood up and shook hands. Mr. Rosenberg left the building, and Scotty walked over to Nancy Gillette and introduced himself.

"Hi! I'm Brian MacTavish. They call me Scotty," he said.

"Hi, I'm Nancy, and they call me Nancy. I own this flying service," she commented.

"Yeah, I know. Mr. Rosenberg told me. He just hired me as a pilot. I'd like to find out if you know of any apartments close to the airport I could rent. I'll be moving here in a few days, and I'll need a place to call home."

Nancy scribbled a name, address, and phone number on a scrap of paper and handed it to him. "It's just a few blocks away. It's a security building with a garage in the basement. They don't require a lot of upfront money or a long lease. It's clean and quiet."

"Thanks, I'll grab a cab right now and see what I can set up. Would you have your line person gas the Cessna for me? I'll be leaving as soon as I get back."

"Consider it done," she answered.

Scotty was back in less than an hour. He had his apartment. Now all he had to do was move. He paid the gas bill and told Nancy he'd see her soon. He went out to the Cessna, did a quick pre-flight walk around, started the engine, and taxied out to the active runway. Thus began the working life of Scotty MacTavish, ferry pilot.

Over the years Scotty and Nancy became good friends. He would taxi over to Gillette to pass a few minutes with Nancy. When one of her planes needed help or a tune up, Scotty would grab his small tool chest and set things right at little or no charge for his time.

CHAPTER NINE

A T THE END OF THE MONTH, Scotty had set himself up in his new apartment and had reported to Aircraft Unlimited bright and early on Monday morning. Ben Rosenberg informed Scotty he would be sending him to a school to learn to fly small to medium-sized jets, but before that his first assignment would be to ferry a twin Beechcraft back from Panama. Ben sent him into town to get the process started to acquire his passport.

When he arrived in Panama and located the Beechcraft he took his time checking the log books, service record, and the aircraft itself. The log book in the aircraft looked clean. Recent service and airworthiness certificates were in order and the aircraft looked to be in reasonable condition, with the exception of the tires.

The right main landing gear tire was well worn and had several radial cracks in the sidewalls. Scotty didn't like it, but the owner refused to put a replacement tire on. Scotty studied the tire again and decided to trust it for one more landing. He signed the papers, filed his flight plan and taxied to the active runway.

When he received takeoff clearance he pulled onto the runway and immediately began his takeoff run. Just before liftoff the right tire blew out. He corrected by using full left aileron to lift the right wing and enough of the right rudder to keep the aircraft moving straight down the runway. By doing these things so quickly, he completed his takeoff without incident.

He climbed to altitude and set his course for Chicago. All the way back he worked scenarios in his mind to make a successful landing in Chicago without bending the airplane too much. By the time he got to the airport, he thought he had a good plan.

When he got within radio range, he switched to the company frequency and asked to speak to Ben. When he answered, Scotty explained what had happened and his plan and asked Ben to talk to the tower people and ask permission to use a grassy area away from the active runway.

Ben asked, "On a scale of one to ten, how confident are you with pulling off this landing?"

"I think a nine without major damage or injury."

"Okay, Scotty. Standby, I'll get right back to you." A few minutes later, "Scotty, I talked to the boss controller. You need to call him as soon as you can."

"I understand, Ben. I'll call right now."

Scotty switched his radio to the tower frequency, called and identified the aircraft. "Scotty, this is Bob Sinclair, the senior controller at this airport. What is it you want to do to get your plane down in one piece?"

Scotty told Bob what he wanted and how he would try to hold the damage down both to the plane and the airport.

"Okay, Scotty, you're the pilot and your plan sounds like a good one. What's your fuel situation?"

"Wing tanks are empty, and less than a quarter of a tank in the auxiliary tank."

"Good, but I have to say, I've never seen this one done before. Here's what I'll suggest you use. To the left of the north runway is an unused taxi strip. To the left of that strip is a wide grassy area. Use that for your runway. I can't tell you how smooth the ground is because I've never been out there.

"You've got a five mile-per-hour wind from three hundred forty-four degrees. It's a little crosswind but shouldn't bother you much. I'll direct the crash crew to the taxi strip, and when they're in position, I'll give you your clearance to land. Now a quick question—are you nervous?"

Scotty chuckled, "Yes, Bob I'm nervous. I've never tried this before but I'm confident it can be done. At the moment, I'm orbiting about ten miles south of the runway."

"Okay, I've cleared all traffic here and the crash crew is in position. You're cleared to land with a straight-in approach. Good luck and fly safe."

Scotty took a deep breath and turned toward the grass runway he would use. At three miles out, he pulled the throttles back and began losing altitude. At two miles out, he lowered the landing gear and dropped to half flaps. At a half mile, he went to full flaps and dropped the nose. He slowed to stall speed, pulled the nose up and added power enough to maintain the slowest speed possible.

He let the plane gently settle down using the left aileron and right rudder to hold the right wing high and the plane tracking straight. Then he brought the power back until the left main gear touched the ground. Still holding the right wing high and right rudder to maintain directional control, he cut the fuel to both engines. Holding the controls steady, he let the speed drop without using brakes.

The nose wheel slowly dropped and settled onto the grass. Now, he used the left brake to hold his direction. Fortunately the ground wasn't too bumpy and directional control wasn't that difficult to hold. By that time he had slowed enough so the ailerons couldn't hold the right wing up anymore. When the right wheel touched the ground, Scotty applied both brakes. In the last ten feet, the plane slowly veered to the right and came to a halt.

He climbed out of the plane and dropped to the ground just as the crash crew pulled up on the taxiway. The medics went directly to Scotty, and the firemen closed in around the plane. No damage to the plane, or the airport, and no damage to the pilot.

Scotty went to the offending tire and checked it out. No damage to the rim but the tire was destroyed. At that moment, he was a very happy person. A week after coming back with the Beech, he was on his way to a flight school in Texas that specialized in jet aircraft training.

One day, after Scotty had landed with a small business jet that Ben had purchased from a Canadian company, he called Scotty into his office and asked, "Would you like to try sales, Scotty?"

"Sure I would, Ben. What have you got in mind?" Scotty answered.

"I have a prospective buyer for that little jet you just brought back. If I get you an appointment with the buyer's pilot, would you fly to Seattle and demonstrate it for me?"

"Absolutely I will. What's the selling price and what am I authorized to do?"

"I've told them the price is $755,000 as is. We'll make no changes. However, we will do a complete safety check of the aircraft and do a search for any changes or updates the factory or the FAA have suggested, if they want us to."

Scotty left the following day for Seattle. The next day he returned to Chicago with a company check for the full price and the information that the buyer would have his people do the checks. They wanted to take possession that day. Ben was happy and Scotty was out of his mind with pleasure. His first attempt at sales had been successful. From that point on, Scotty became one of three pilot salesmen for Aircraft Unlimited.

About this time, Ben Rosenberg opened his hangers as a general aviation service facility. He hired the very best mechanics he could find and bought the very best equipment for that service department. Almost immediately it became a success. They built an engine overhaul room that could have been used as a hospital clean room.

One day, as Scotty was bringing another twin Beech Craft back to Chicago, it came to him that he had no personal life. This had to change. He was stale. He hadn't taken a vacation since he started with Aircraft Unlimited and that was four years ago. He wanted to see his parents and visit with friends. Kim had finished college and planned to marry Jack Stubblefield in the fall. He decided to take an extended vacation at the same time.

Maybe Dad and Mom would like to go fishing after the wedding, he thought. As soon as he landed, he called Kim to verify the date of the wedding. Then he went into Ben's office and asked for two months off.

"Great idea. I've been worried about you. I don't want you pushing yourself so hard. You'll burn out," Ben said. "In fact, we'll keep you on the payroll the second month and you can spend your time scouting for aircraft we can pick up," he continued.

It was during the second month of his vacation that Scotty found a 1947 Beechcraft Bonanza with aircraft license number N3211V. He had called on an ad in the local paper for sale, 1947 Beechcraft Bonanza in good flying condition. It was hiding in a tee hanger on a farm in northern Minnesota. She was a little worse for wear with her red-and-white faded paint, threadbare seats, side panels, and carpeting. But, it was love at first sight.

The owner had purchased her new. Scotty negotiated with the owner, they arrived at a price, and he wrote a personal check and the deal was done. He left his car in the farmer's yard and said he would pick it up the next day.

He did a thorough pre-flight of the whole plane then started the engine. Everything looked good so he taxied to the grass runway right next to the barn and flew the Bonanza back to Boerger's flight service.

For the next two years, Scotty gathered parts and materials until he had a good portion of what he thought he would need. Then he spent most of his free time at Boerger's flight service, renovating and upgrading the old Bonanza. When he had two or more days off or during his vacations he would fly to Minneapolis, stay with his parents, and work on the Bonanza. He did all the work on the plane himself. All of the engine work had been completed at Aircraft Unlimited engine overhaul shop.

Scotty installed new interior fabric, custom seats with adjustable vertical as well as fore and aft movement, a new single nav-com radio, new paint, new tires and brakes, a renovated electrical system, an updated fuel system incorporating an electric fuel pump, and an overhauled retractable landing gear system. In short, she was better than new. She was beautiful, and Scotty was really in love.

During a conversation with Len and Buster, Len suggested an emergency survival kit similar to the type bush pilots carried. "Who knows what might happen or what you might need in an emergency," Len commented.

"That's true," Buster added. "I've heard a lot of stories about downed pilots living off the land or repairing a damaged airplane using something out of their survival kit."

Then Scotty asked, "What kind of things do you put in a survival kit?"

"That depends on the type of terrain you'll be flying over most of the time," Len answered. "Here in Minnesota, I'd carry a good first aid kit, a small set of tools, spare spark plugs, some dried food, fresh water, one of those small backpacker's butane camp stoves, a small cooking pan, matches, sleeping bag, and probably, a .22-caliber break-down rifle. Oh, yes, and the most important article, an emergency portable radio. Did I forget anything, Buster?"

"The only thing I'd add would be some warm clothes during the fall and winter months," Buster added.

Scotty added a survival kit to his list of things for the Bonanza. He also added candy bars, crackers, and a surplus US Navy flare pistol and a full box of flares.

He called in the federal inspectors. They looked her over, checked the log book entries and gave her a clean bill of health. He took her up several times for short flights to make sure everything worked. Then he loaded her up and flew her to Chicago and her new home, a private hanger a few doors down from Aircraft Unlimited.

It was about this time that Ben Rosenberg decided the business was ready to expand again. He called a staff meeting and asked each of his employees to make suggestions as to what part of the country he should consider for the second major step in the company's expansion.

Scotty stepped forward with Minneapolis/St Paul as the most likely expansion area because of the exploding electronics and medical businesses. There should be a real probability of corporate charter flights and purchasing aircraft in the four largest cities of Minneapolis, St. Paul, Rochester, and Duluth.

After reviewing Scotty's proposal and several others, Ben agreed with Scotty and asked him to get proposals on possible hanger and office space at one of the airports. Within a few weeks, Scotty had a spot located at Flying Cloud Airport, located in the southwestern suburb of Eden Prairie.

Ben then asked Scotty, "Would you like to try being the first manager of our new Minneapolis office?"

With a big grin on his face, Scotty answered, "I'd love to. I'll give it my best shot, and I don't think you'll need a second manager."

"That's a great attitude. I want you to make your recommendations for the new offices and tell me what you'll need to make it a positive attraction for the flying public," Ben ordered.

After the grand opening of the second Aircraft Unlimited location late Sunday, Ben and Scotty retired to the office. Ben congratulated Scotty on a good beginning and then added, "I want you to fly down to Santa Cruz, Bolivia, within the next few days. I found a flyable Ford tri-motor down there, and I have a collector that's been looking for one for several years. I want you to look it over really good. If you're comfortable with its condition, fly it to Chicago. I'll call the owner tomorrow and ask about training. You're the only pilot we have with a chance to get this bird back in one piece. As soon as I can find the answer to training, I'll fax you the information. I do have the contact person's name," Ben responded.

A day and a half later, Scotty boarded a commercial flight to Santa Cruz, Bolivia. Three days after that, Scotty had checked out the plane, the deal had been signed, and he had completed six hours of duel instruction.

The old Ford had seen better days. She had served as a passenger airliner in the United States for many years and passenger and freight-liner in Bolivia. All of the systems worked and someone had updated the control surface cables by moving them inside and out of the weather. All of the control surfaces moved smoothly and easily.

During his review of the aircraft log books and service reports he discovered that all three engines had been replaced with newer, more economical, but yet more powerful versions of the original engines.

The old tri-motor was equipped for instrument flying, but all of the instruments dated from the 1940s and 1950s. So, he didn't want a lot of over water flying in bad weather and his tentative flight plan called for a lot of over water miles.

The last leg of this journey would be to Chicago. Depending on how he felt, he may stop somewhere in between to rest. The trip was 1,300 miles, and that would get him into Chicago late at night. At least he would be able to find an airport he could land at. *That's not a bad idea at all,* he thought.

The following morning, Scotty appeared at the airport to begin the trip to Chicago. He did his pre-flight inspection of the outside of the old Ford, then opened the cabin door and climbed into the plane. He was astonished to see the whole cabin filled with spare parts including a spare engine. He rushed back to the airport office and called the former owner. "Where did all these parts come from?" he asked.

"They're all of the spare parts we had for this last tri-motor in our flying inventory, and they're all new parts. Don't worry, they won't overload you. We could have packed all three engines into the plane if we had them. They could come in handy if she gets cranky.

When he reached his prescribed altitude he pulled the throttles back to economy cruise power and set his course for the first refueling stop—Quito, Ecuador. *Boy, I'm amazed at how well this old Ford is performing with the load she's carrying. This old girl is making a little less than ninety miles per hour over the ground. I must have picked up a head wind,* Scotty thought.

The following morning, he checked all of the fuel tanks. They were all topped up nicely. He drained a little from each tank to check for contaminants. There were none. He checked the oil level in all three engines. He was satisfied that it was safe to begin this second leg.

At 6:00 a.m. the following day, the tri-motor lifted away from the San Salvador runway and headed north to New Orleans, USA, 1,000 miles away. So far the old Ford had been just great. She handled well, and the engines had been humming the same tune all the way. However, Scotty did have to manipulate the throttles to keep the engines in sync.

At about two hours south of New Orleans the right engine began losing rpms. Scotty heard the reduction first and then began to see it on the tachometer. "Okay, Miss Ford, what's up with this now? Are you just trying to keep me on the edge of my seat because we're over water?" Scotty muttered. He checked the few engine instruments the Ford had but couldn't identify any problem with that engine. "Probably spark plugs," he said to himself.

"According to your operations manual, you should be able to maintain altitude on two engines with a full gross load. As long as we are not at full gross, I should be able to throttle back your sick engine and make it to New Orleans just a few minutes late. Let's give it a try," he offered the old Ford.

Slowly, he reduced power to the right engine. He made adjustments to the flight controls to correct the yaw induced by the left engine. During this process, Scotty watched the altimeter and airspeed indicators. Altitude didn't move but airspeed dropped about three miles per hour. "Will you look at this. The manual is right for a change? You still have the power, old girl. We'll make New Orleans on two engines as long as my left leg doesn't get tired holding this much pressure on the rudder."

When Scotty was satisfied that he was going to continue flying, he picked up his microphone and called, "New Orleans Approach Control, this is Charlie Paul one three niner four four."

A moment later, "Charlie Paul one three niner four four, this is New Orleans Control. Go ahead."

"New Orleans, I'm on a VFR flight to New Orleans. I am twenty minutes out at eighty-eight miles an hour airspeed. I'm flying a Ford Tri-motor with one engine shut down. There's no fire and the engine could be re-started for a short period of time if it becomes necessary. I am not, repeat, not declaring an emergency. I am able to maintain altitude and reasonable airspeed. I will advise you if the situation changes."

"Three niner four four, your situation has been noted. Report on New Orleans Tower frequency when you are fifteen minutes out and turn your landing lights on, if you have them. Control, out."

"Roger New Orleans."

At the appointed fifteen minutes, Scotty called New Orleans Tower. He was given current weather and a straight in approach to the active runway. He slowed to approach speed and when he passed over the end of the runway, he flared and greased a three-point landing. He carefully applied brakes to slow the tri-motor down and turned off the active runway at the first intersection. He picked up his microphone and called, "New Orleans ground control, this is tri-motor Charlie Paul one three niner four four. Could you give me taxi instructions to a general aviation service facility?"

When Scotty came out of the cockpit, he saw a man in coveralls coming through the cabin door. He said, "Hi, I'm Rod. I'm the chief mechanic here. What seems to be the problem with this antique?"

"Hi, Rod, I'm Scotty. This antique is one sweet aircraft. I'm ferrying it for Aircraft Unlimited to Chicago. "I'm a licensed A&E myself and if it wouldn't be too much of a problem, I'd like to work on it with you. And if you don't have the parts, I probably have them somewhere in these boxes."

"You're Scotty MacTavish, that genius kid who got his A&E licenses before he graduated from high school? Is it true, you never missed a question?"

Scotty looked a little sheepish, "Yah, that's me," he answered.

After the tri-motor was pushed into a corner, a short balding man approached Scotty. "I'm from Customs. Can I see your papers and cargo manifest?"

Scotty pulled his papers out of his pocket and said, "I don't have a cargo manifest. All I have are spare parts for this airplane. Please feel free to rummage through the boxes in the cabin. We'll probably be here until morning."

He looked into the cabin and commented as he walked away, "I'll be back in a few minutes." A few minutes later he returned with another man and a dog. They took the dog into the plane and went through it very carefully.

"I know. I was escorted part way in by the Air Force. They had a terrible time trying to match my eighty-eight miles an hour. They didn't stay with me very long. Those war birds don't like slow speeds all that well."

After about thirty minutes the Customs person returned Scotty's papers to him and walked away without a word.

By 4:00 a.m. the following morning, the Ford was running like a brand-new airplane and Scotty had six more friends in New Orleans. At 9:00 a.m., after a few hours sleep, he fired up the engines and let them warm up as he taxied out to the active runway. He waited in line at the end of the runway, behind a 747 and a Lear, for his turn to take off. When the tower gave him his take off clearance he acknowledged with a request, "I'd like permission for an immediate left turn out of the pattern? This thing isn't the fastest bird on the field and I want to get out of the way as soon as I can."

"Ford tri-motor, permission granted for immediate left turn at your discretion. Have a safe flight and take good care of that tin goose."

Scotty advanced all three throttles and began singing, "Off we go into the wild blue yonder, flying high, into the sky." Within 100 yards he was airborne and beginning his turn out of the pattern.

While he climbed, he set his course for Chicago and settled back in the seat to enjoy the ride and scenery in a low, slow fifteen-hour flight through the American heartland. He was happy.

At a little after 2:00 p.m. he decided he'd had enough. He caught himself closing his eyes. In this aircraft, that could be a fatal mistake. He was just too tired to continue. He changed his flight plan to land in St. Louis. He needed sleep, a shower, and a hot meal.

By the time he checked in, showered and dressed in clean clothes it was almost 6:00 p.m. He went down to the restaurant and had dinner, ordering a big T-bone steak rare along with all the normal fixings. At 8:00 p.m. he was back in his room and fell sound asleep.

At six the next morning, he was sitting in line behind an American Airlines 727 waiting his turn. When it came, he again requested an immediate turn out of the pattern to get away from faster traffic. His request was granted and he was on his way to completing his last leg

When he taxied up to the Aircraft Unlimited hangers, all three buildings emptied to watch. Scotty shut down the engines, entered his comments into the log book right behind the entries of the repairs he had done at New Orleans.

The flight line crew chocked the wheels and opened the cabin door. Ben entered the cabin and his jaw dropped. He asked, "Damn, Scotty, what in hell are all these parts?"

"They came with the plane, Ben. And I thank the Lord we had them. I had a rough engine coming into New Orleans. I landed there to find out why. You know me, Ben, mister safety first. I wasn't sure what the problem was, so I needed to dig into it and make it right. I didn't want to bend this nice airplane. So, with some help from a crew of very nice people, we replaced a magneto and spark plugs out of our spare parts. The rest of the trip was a downright pleasure. All three engines are running like a dream.

"I turn it over to you, with my thanks for giving me this trip. I don't think I have ever enjoyed a trip as much as this one, even if it was long. This old bird is great. Even with that load of parts, she flew just fine on two engines. I had complete control on the flight in and during landing. If your customer doesn't want her, I just might make an offer on her myself.

Ben asked if the log-book was up to date and did he had included the repairs at New Orleans?"

"Yes and yes," Scotty answered.

"I should have known. Well, when you get back, take a few days off. You've earned it," Ben answered.

CHAPTER TEN

SCOTTY'S EYES FLEW OPEN WHEN A SHUDDER RACKED his body. He used his good right arm to pull the sleeve of his suit coat up. He winced from the pain but managed to see his watch. It was smashed. So was the instrument panel clock. It was still daylight but the fog was creating a false feeling of night.

The ground squirrels and birds were coming back. Big birds, small birds, cold black ravens, and crows all entered the area. He saw several deer directly across the small clearing and listened to the chattering of the red squirrels. It was almost pleasant to listen to this wildlife.

He pulled his coat back around his shoulders. The cold wasn't the primary problem now. It was the pain in his arm and both his legs. His stomach was still squeamish and started to ache. Depression was increasing. His thoughts switched to Grace and little Billy. He began to talk, "I didn't mean this to happen. Grace, forgive me. This isn't what I wanted. You and Billy are all I care for. I wanted to be there for both of you."

His head dropped to his chest and he began to weep. In his mind, the outlook was very dark. He stayed in this position for several minutes, then his head popped up and his back straightened. He Shouted. "NO!!! I'm not going to go down without a fight. I owe that much to myself," He shouted again, "Lord, help me to find a way. Please give me the strength to think this thing through. There has to be a way to get help."

He closed his eyes and let his thoughts go to finding an answer. His mind was totally jumbled. He tried to straighten it out. He needed to get to the luggage compartment. He had to leave the comfort and protection of the cockpit. His warm clothes were in that luggage compartment along with his flare pistol, flares and night was beginning to set in.

"Maybe I can get these things and then crawl back inside to the radio. Or bring the microphone outside with me, if it will reach that far. I need to think this thing through before I start."

Now his mind was clearing. It moved from one point to another with lightning speed. He couldn't take the plane's radio out with him but he had the portable emergency radio. Why didn't he think of that sooner? He reached into the side pocket of the passenger's seat and removed the portable radio.

He looked out the side window and was surprised to see the fog thinning again. He looked straight up to see rips in the fog. He could see blue sky through those rips.

He emptied his map case of everything and then dropped the portable radio into the bottom. He pulled his bloody topcoat off his shoulders and pushed it into the map case. He looked around the cockpit. What else would I need if I couldn't get back into the cockpit? *"Yes, my water and the first aid kit. I'll need them,"* he thought.

He was worn out. The pain was taking a lot out of him and his stomach was really hurting now. He couldn't or wouldn't take any painkillers because of his bleeding. He pulled the topcoat out of the map case and arranged it across his chest and over his legs.

He needed some rest before he began his trek outside. He gently allowed his head to rest against the side window. Maybe it would help his headache.

CHAPTER ELEVEN

S COTTY WAS EXHAUSTED AND SLEPT most of the trip back to the Twin Cities after dropping of the tri-engine in Chicago. When the cab arrived at his apartment, he flopped onto his bed without taking off his clothes. After a good nights sleep in his own bed, Scotty decided to take his beloved Bonanza out for a short hop. He loaded his gear, and gave the plane a close pre-flight because he hadn't flown it in a few weeks. He found nothing wrong or even suspicious. But then he hadn't expected anything either.

He got into the cockpit and started the engine. He listened to the current weather briefing and ground control information while the engine warmed up. He set his altimeter to the barometer reading he received from the weather broadcast, and then he picked up the microphone. "Flying Cloud ground control, this is Bonanza three two one one victor, with weather information. Request taxi instructions for a west bound departure."

"One victor, Flying Cloud ground, cleared to taxi to runway two seven left and hold."

"One victor."

He opened the throttle a little and began taxiing to runway two seven left. While he taxied, he did his engine pre-flight checks and made sure all his controls were working properly. By the time he reached the end of the runway, he was ready for takeoff. He switched to the tower frequency and called, "Flying Cloud tower, this is Bonanza three two one one victor at two seven left requesting takeoff clearance west bound."

"One victor, I have a Musketeer on short final. As soon as he's past you, taxi into position and hold for clearance."

Scotty clicked the mike switch twice to acknowledge the tower's instruction.

He watched the Musketeer flare out and make a perfect landing. Then he taxied onto the runway and waited for clearance. He watched the Musketeer exit the active runway at the first turn off.

One victor, you are cleared for takeoff west bound. You, and that beautiful Beech, have a good flight."

"Thanks, Neal. One victor, rolling."

Scotty let the Bonanza fly when it was ready and slowly climbed to a low cruising altitude. He put a cassette into the tape machine, turned down the volume and settled back in his seat. He picked up his microphone and called, "Minneapolis Flight Service, this is Bonanza three two one one victor."

"Go ahead one victor."

"Minneapolis, I'd like to file a flight plan to Rapid City, via Willmar. Estimated flight time three hours fifty-two minutes. Pilot Brian MacTavish. Time off, 0955 local."

"Roger, one victor. Flight plan activated. Minneapolis, out."

Scotty brought the volume back up on the tape machine and listened to the Dixieland music of Pete Fountain. Three hours and fifty-one minutes later his wheels touched down on the Rapid City airport runway. He canceled his flight plan and taxied to the transit parking area and went into the administration building for lunch. Forty minutes later, with a full belly and full fuel tanks, he reversed the whole program and returned to Flying Cloud.

As he parked the Bonanza in the Aircraft Unlimited hanger, he commented to no one in particular, "Now that's a bus man's holiday if I ever heard of one. Fly from Minneapolis to Bolivia to Chicago to Minneapolis. Get a good nights rest and fly to Rapid City and back for lunch. I think something is missing."

After supper that evening, he called his sister. "Kim, how do I go about meeting eligible young ladies? Maybe it's time I begin thinking about settling down. At the least making an effort to find a female roommate, wife, or a female friend that can help me get my mind off flying. Or, how about one that likes to travel on a low budget? Any ideas?"

Kim let out a loud cackling laugh that pierced through the phone lines like a knife.

"What? I'm being serious here, Kim. Don't laugh. I need some serious help. I've never been into this dating thing, and I don't know where to begin. Please, give me a little help. If you'll remember, I gave you some much needed help when you got yourself in a little too deep back in school," Scotty whined.

"Yeah, I remember. I'm sorry big brother. I shouldn't have laughed so loud, but you sounded so, I don't know, so lost, up tight and kind of afraid maybe. Well, let's see what we can come up with. There's always the get acquainted or personals columns in the paper. Maybe the church has a singles group.

"There's always the dating services. There are several of those, but whatever you do, don't get into the bar scene. That's usually a dead end and a very expensive way to go. Besides, you don't drink so you'd be wasting your time," Kim said.

"How about some of your school friends? Are any of them still single?"

Kim was silent for a few seconds and then commented, "I don't think so but let me do some checking. You could always use that charm you have to work some magic on your female flying friends. I thought you had a girl back in Chicago. What happened to her?"

"She couldn't handle being alone so often, or for so long. She found someone else to take her out when I had to go out of town. I'll have to say it wasn't a big loss for either of us. We didn't get along that well anyway. She liked to party hardy and I couldn't always do that."

They continued their conversation for a few more minutes and He said, "Kim, let me think this situation over for a while and we'll talk again." He put the phone on its cradle, put his feet up on the desk, and thought about what Kim had said to him. *This may not be as easy as I had thought.*

Later that day, Scotty was taking a turn through the hanger locking doors, checking aircraft for fluid leaks, and turning out lights. The phone began its incessant ringing echoing through the quiet hanger with a violence that assaulted his eardrums. He ran to his office and snatched the phone from its cradle, "Aircraft Unlimited, this is Brian."

CHAPTER TWELVE

EARLY ON A MONDAY MORNING, Ben called Scotty and told him to hire and train a secretary for his office. "Over the next two or three months, you may be doing a lot of traveling," Ben warned. "I have several deals working right now and it'll probably require several overseas trips for you. Some of these could be extended trips and we can't afford to close your shop for that long. We could, and probably would, lose business," Ben advised.

"I'll put an ad in the paper, Ben. It shouldn't take more than a few weeks to find and train someone," Scotty said.

"If these deals turn hot, you may not have a few weeks, but do the best you can. I'll call you in a few days." With that, Ben broke the connection.

Scotty sat, quietly, for a few minutes, then went to the files and pulled out the paperwork on one of the first sales he had made out of this office. He had sold a nice little Piper Tri-pacer to the owner of an employment agency. *Why not give him a chance to fill the position?* He thought. He picked up the phone and dialed the number.

"Jim, this is Scotty MacTavish."

"Scotty, it's good to hear from you. What can I do for my favorite airplane salesman?"

"I thought I'd give you a chance to fill an opening here at the shop," Scotty said. "I'm going to need a good secretary. Someone I can trust to be here on time every day. The work needs to get done even if I'm not here. It would be nice if she had some experience in the aircraft industry, but it isn't completely necessary." They discussed wages, if Scotty would be paying the placement fee, and other details.

"Let me look through our listings," Jim said. "I'll call you with candidates. It shouldn't be too hard to find someone."

"Great. I'll be looking forward to hearing from you," Scotty responded.

The following morning, Jim called with three candidates he wanted to send out. He gave Scotty a quick synopsis of all three.

"They sound qualified, Jim. Make appointments with all three for tomorrow starting at 8:00 a.m. the next one at 10:00 a.m. and the last one at 1:00 p.m. I should make a hiring decision by tomorrow afternoon," Scotty promised.

"I'll set it up," Jim said. "Scotty, thanks for the opportunity to help."

"By the way, how's the tri-pacer doing?" Scotty asked.

"It's flying like a bird. I took the wife and son to Duluth last weekend and we had a wonderful flight and a wonderful weekend. Thanks for asking." Jim said.

"The next time you're going out flying with the family, give me a call here at the hanger. If I'm in town, I'd love to meet your wife and son."

"I'll do that, Scotty."

Scotty made a list of three questions he would ask each woman. How much do you know about the aviation industry? Why do you think you want to work for an aircraft service and sales company? Would you be interested in travel or sales? He felt that these questions would give him a good idea of where each applicant was headed.

The first applicant walked in the door two minutes before eight the following morning. Her name was Mary-Beth Rogers. She was in her mid-twenties, well dressed and carried herself in an aggressive manner. She didn't have a resume to give him, so she told him she had a BA degree in History, was married and had two children. She said her husband had helped her with her degree and he taught high school history in one of the southern suburbs. She answered all three of his questions in a short, curt and aggressive manner. "Nothing" to question one, because it sounds interesting to question 2, and yes to question 3." She would be in the running but not really what he was looking for.

The second applicant walked in at exactly 10:00 a.m. She introduced herself as Grace Johnson and handed him a neatly typed resume. She was a very well-dressed, attractive woman with reddish-blond hair and very little makeup. He liked that. She sat quietly while he scanned the single page resume. He looked at her with a smile on his face and commented, "Your resume is very well done. It answers two of my question right off the bat."

"I'm happy to hear that, Mr. MacTavish. I created it last night after I had researched your company."

"I'm impressed that you took the time to become familiar with the company. I see you have a business degree and I see an office management position and a few years as an airline stewardess. Do you like the aircraft industry?"

"Yes, I really enjoy everything about the industry, but I don't like the problems that come with being a stewardess with a major carrier. It sometimes gets very intense."

"Do you mind telling me what those problems are?"

"At this time, yes I do mind."

"I understand, Miss Johnson. No need to worry about it. It's really none of my business anyway. I was just curious because I ride the airlines quite frequently. Let's continue. I have only one question left. Why do you want to work for a relatively small service and sales company?"

"In my research of your company, I saw you have expanded twice in less than two years. Both of them classified as major expansions. That tells me you have intelligent, stable management and are successful and growing. I'd like to be a part of that growth."

"Very well put, Miss Johnson. If you are the successful candidate, when could you start?"

"At any time you choose, Mr. MacTavish."

"I thank you for coming in. This has been a very interesting interview. I'll be talking with Jim and making a decision later this afternoon." After she had left, Scotty commented to the empty room, *Now, that's the kind of person I need in this office.* She showed him absolutely no nonsense and was very professional. He locked up the office and went to lunch. His next interview was ninety minutes away.

Scotty was standing in front of his office window gazing out at the beautiful day. At five minutes before one o'clock a car entered the parking lot and parked at the back of the lot. It was a fairly new all-white Cadillac sedan. He thought it might be a client for an airplane, but nobody got out of the car. He kept watching and finally a woman got out and began walking toward the office. He looked at the clock. It was one minute before one o'clock. He smiled and walked into the outer office.

She introduced herself as Rhonda Kline and she also had a completed resume. He invited her to sit down in the chair opposite the receptionist's desk and scanned it quickly. He found out she was married, had no children and is currently the office manager for a very successful realty office. She was twenty-nine years old. *My guess is she wants more out of life then what she's getting*, he thought. He asked her about her experience in aviation.

"I don't have any experience in aviation. In fact I don't know anything at all about an airplane. She continued, "I just want to get out of the real estate business. I know it pays good but here's the deal. I'm married to the guy that owns the company see. And he thinks I don't know when he's runnin' around on me and I need a job so I can divorce the SOB."

Scotty sat back and let his mind think this lady through. *This is not what I want. How can I gracefully get out of this interview,* "Well, Mrs. Kline, I think you may have wasted your time applying for this position. I need someone who has some knowledge of the aircraft business. In fact it's now imperative that the person sitting at this desk have that knowledge. Because that person will be on her own. Sometimes that could be for many days when I'm out of the country. I'm truly sorry that Jim didn't tell you that."   "He told me but I thought I'd try anyway. Thanks for seeing me though." She grabbed her resume from the desk and walked out of the door.

After the door closed, Scotty laughed very hard for at least two minutes. By the end of the day, he had made his decision. He dialed Jim's number and when he came on the line Scotty said, "Jim you sent me three almost perfect candidates. I would like to offer the position to Grace Johnson. She's the one who has a BA degree in business and has airline experience. She's not working now, and she told me she could start as soon as we wanted her. I want her bright and early Monday morning. Do I call her and make the offer or do you?" Scotty asked.

"We can do it either way. I'll need her to come into my office anyway, so why don't I do it. I have the benefit package and she was okay with the pay. Now, where do you want the invoice to go?"

"Send it to me. I'll cut the check and have it in the mail by the end of next week. Thanks for the quick response, Jim."

Scotty broke the connection and sat back in his chair. "With a little luck this could be the start of something very nice," he commented to the empty room.

Grace Johnson walked into the hanger office at exactly 8:00 a.m. Monday morning. Her attitude was positive. She had told her roommate, a stewardess with the same airline Grace had worked for, that this job looked like a great opportunity to grow with the company. Besides, the manager was a great looking guy and seemed very down to earth even if he was a pilot. And as far as Grace was concerned, pilots couldn't be trusted once they were out of sight.

The first thing Scotty explained were the wide responsibilities he wanted her to accept as the office manager, including sales and marketing when he was out of town. He showed her how to access the computer-based inventory of all equipment at their location and how to access the company-wide inventory of aircraft for sale. The office financial software she was already familiar with, so he didn't go into that.

"These are the two most important sources of information for you to learn. It'll be your responsibility to help any potential customer if I'm out of the office," Scotty told her. At 9:45 a.m. he took her out on the hanger floor and gave her a quick tour with explanations of the entire flying inventory.

"How about that Beechcraft parked by the front door?" Grace asked. "You haven't said anything about that one."

"That's my personal aircraft and someday, when we have some time I'll tell you about it. I'll tell you that I have completely renovated this plane and it's a lot more safe and comfortable then a brand new Bonanza." He explained. "In fact, do you have anything going tonight?

Please understand, I'm not asking for a date or anything. However, we need to introduce you to people at the home office in Chicago and if you wouldn't mind a long first day, we can go there today. That way you'll get an idea of what you will be doing for me and this company."

Grace looked at him with an un-asked question in her eyes. "No I don't have anything I need to be home for this evening. However, I will need to let my roommate know I'll be late. We kind of, look out for each other."

"Great! Make your call and we'll fly down right now," he said.

Grace went into her new office and Scotty walked over to the wall switch and opened the hanger door in front of the Bonanza. He hooked the tow bar to the nose wheel and pulled the Bonanza onto the apron. He did a quick walk around, checked the oil and drained a little fuel out of each wing tank and the reserve tank to check for contaminants.

Scotty returned the tow bar to its place and locked the service door. Grace came out of the office and said, "I guess I'm ready."

He shut off all the lights in the hanger and they walked out into the sunshine. On his way out, he pushed the switch to close the big hanger door.

"The Bonanza only has one door into the cabin," Scotty explained. "You'll have to climb onto the wing and into your seat by yourself. Just be careful where and how you step. Watch where I step and follow what I do."

When they were both seated, Scotty showed Grace the proper way to adjust the seat belts. Then he felt really stupid. Surely, a former stewardess would know how to adjust a seat belt. His faced flushed when he realized what he had done. To cover his embarrassment, he twisted the radio dials to the weather briefing channel and listened to the litany of information on wind speed and direction, altimeter setting, temperature, visibility, and ceiling.

When he was satisfied, Scotty started the engine and reached across Grace to close and lock the cockpit door. Fifteen minutes later they were in the air.

Scotty hadn't planned on taking Grace to Chicago this soon. He had planned it after two or three weeks. Then he would send her there to meet everyone. He didn't realize the significance of this spur-of-the-moment trip. It was because he wanted to spend more time with her alone in his flying world. In fact, he didn't realize he had been smitten by her charms. He hadn't even admitted to himself that she was a beautiful woman.

After Scotty had attained his planned altitude, he set up the auto pilot for its first setting to home on the Rockford beacon. He turned his attention to Grace. "I'd like to ask you a few questions and I'd like to have your honest answer or opinion. First let me say that you are a very attractive woman, and some men may not trust you to know all about airplanes. Keep in mind I'm out of town a lot of the time. How would you handle a possible client?"

"My first question would be what the primary use of the aircraft would be. If he couldn't give a straight answer to that question, I'd try to show him light planes possibly a two-place like a Piper or a Cessna."

"Ben will ask you questions like this. Give him an honest answer, and you'll be great. He respects all his people and he'll never degrade you for something you don't know about. I have a few books about airplanes at home that could help you with that part of your job. I know a little of your background and this should be a perfect fit for you. I don't think any man could say no to any suggestion you might make, and that's including me."

When they arrived, Scotty parked the Bonanza close to the hanger. A flight line attendant came out and put chocks around the wheels. He then offered his hand to Grace as she stepped down off the wing. He introduced himself and welcomed her to Chicago and to the Aircraft Unlimited family. "Scotty, Ben's waiting in his office to see you."

Scotty introduced her to everyone on the hanger floor. Then they climbed the stairs to the balcony offices. He introduced her to Ben's secretary, Suzy Turner. "Suzy will be your best source of information until you get accustomed to our way of doing things," he told Grace.

"Ben's on the phone right now," Suzy said. "Grace, it's about time you showed up here, welcome. We'll be talking a lot over the next few months. Ben's always coming up with new ideas or sending Scotty off into the boonies somewhere in the world and it's up to us to make sure everything is coordinated."

"I think I'm going to like this job," Grace commented. "It sounds like it won't get boring anytime soon."

Suzy noticed Ben had completed his call. She pushed the intercom button and announced, "Ben, Scotty and Grace Johnson, his new office manager, are here."

"Great! All of you come in right away, and Suzy, bring coffee." Ben warmly welcomed Grace to the Aircraft Unlimited family and motioned them to a round conference table. For the next two hours they discussed the company's philosophy and the future Ben had envisioned. He told Scotty to take Grace out to dinner on the company, as soon as they got back. That was to reward her for putting up with his long-winded informational meeting and for the long first day she had endured.

Scotty and Grace walked slowly out to the Bonanza. "I hope you now have some idea of what it's like to work for Ben and this company. It's kind of like a large family. We all get along very well and Ben will reward you for everything you do for him and the company. You are a beautiful and very intelligent woman and you will go a long way in the growth of this organization, and I hope you never leave me."

Grace took a minute to organize her thoughts and then in a little slightly quivering voice said; "All I can tell you at this time, that I will do my very best to help you grow this office in every way I can. I'm impressed with every one I've met today they're all so helpful. I just can't believe this is real."

"It's real all right, believe me." Scotty said.

Jimmy, one of the young line boys came running up to them and informed Scotty, "I topped up all three tanks and checked the oil. It's all good, but I checked your plane log and you'll need a top end on the engine right after your next oil change."

"Thanks, Jimmy. Inform the engine shop will you?"

Jimmy waved just as Scotty hopped up on the wing and then helped Grace up. Grace thanked him and he waved to her then removed all three wheel chocks. He ran out in front of the plane so Scotty could see him.

Scotty opened the side and called, "Clear," and stated the engine. As soon as he was satisfied everything was a go, called the tower for weather and taxi clearance to the active runway. As they taxied, Scotty did his controls and engine checks and pulled up third in line for takeoff. While they waited, Scotty asked, "What kind of music do you like?"

Grace answered, "Soft music. Something like Swan Lake or some of the light classics. Now that's a great way to relax after a hard day."

"This is something else I put in this plane." He pushed a few buttons and soft classic music of Swan Lake came into the cockpit and mixed with the engine. Scotty leaned back in his seat, engaged the auto pilot and closed his eyes. Grace look at him with a broad smile on her face then leaned back and closed her eyes.

Over the next year, Grace and Scotty formed a close working relationship and friendship. Scotty still traveled a lot, and Grace became a good sales person. In that first year she was instrumental in three separate major sales at a good profit for the company. Ben was so impressed that he gave her a nice bonus and a significant pay increase.

Scotty decided that he should do something for her, also. So, he took her out to dinner and to a show—in New York. That was when their friendship changed into something much more personal. Scotty was in love again, and this time it wasn't an airplane. Six months later Grace did something she told her roommate she would never do, especially with a pilot. She moved into Scotty's apartment. Six months later they were married.

The wedding was huge. It took place in Grace's hometown of Superior, Wisconsin, and Bong Airfield had more different types of aircraft parked on the ramps, in the grass, and along a rarely used taxi strip than ever before. The wedding took place on Saturday morning and the parties lasted until Sunday morning. The last aircraft took off from Bong Field at 3:30 p.m. It was a Lear jet with a flight plan to Stockholm, Sweden, and piloted by Scotty.

They arrived in Stockholm very early in the morning. Scotty made arrangements for hanger space and servicing the Lear. Their hotel had a car and driver waiting to take their luggage and them for a much needed rest.

They spent a week seeing the sites of Stockholm. They even took a trip into the mountains. They spend several days calling on Grace's family still living in Sweden, and Scotty made several courtesy calls to Ben's friends and customers. There last day was spent shopping for souvenirs of this trip, and some clothes that Scotty had forgotten to pack.

The next day the Lear took off for Norway, and a short time latter they landed at a small airstrip in Oslo. More of Grace's family waited at the airstrip to welcome their cousin and her new husband. Scotty made arrangements for the refueling and hanger space for a two-night stay.

When all the welcomes had been said, everyone went to their cars and proceeded to the grand uncle's home, located on the outskirts of Oslo. Once they entered through the large iron gate held in place by a seven-foot high iron fence they drove at least five minutes and rounded a small mountain that revealed a large brick-and-stone castle. Surrounding the castle on three sides were five smaller buildings that looked like they could be guest houses.

On what appeared to Scotty to be the down wind side of these buildings, and about two hundred yards away were a large barn and several smaller outbuildings. There was a fenced in area that looked like it might be a work out area for training horses.

Grand Aunty told Grace to take her new husband through a covered walkway to the guest house to rest and relax. Dinner would be served at eight that evening, and dress would be semi-formal.

The following morning, one of the hired hands returned them to town and the hotel where reservations had been made for them. They spent that day doing what visitors did—shopping and watching the locals rushing around. They visited a small museum of musical instruments, and looked and listened to music of Norway. Scotty bought six records of classical Norwegian music to add to his collection in his Bonanza. That evening they had a sea food feast at the hotel's restaurant.

The next morning at 6:00 a.m. local time, Scotty and Grace were waiting in line to take off on their next experience in Finland, Denmark, Germany, Switzerland, France, Scotland, England, Ireland, and several of the Near East countries. From that point on there wouldn't be any relatives involved. The only reason to go to any of them was to show them to Grace. Scotty had been in most of them more then once. This would be a sight-seeing trip only.

Before they realized it, the Lear touched down at Flying Cloud Airport again, and sixty days had fallen from the calendar.

With Grace's help, Scotty continued to grow the business at Flying Cloud Airport. His log book had many thousands of hours in many different aircraft types. From the beginning, he had kept a second log book of all of the airports and countries he had flown to. It was amazing even to him. The only countries he hadn't visited were the communist countries and only then because Ben wouldn't do business with them. Even that could change now that the cold war was winding down. Ben might change his mind.

CHAPTER THIRTEEN

I T WAS ONLY A FEW MINUTES THAT SCOTTY SLEPT, but he woke up in a more positive mood. The headache and pain problems still plagued him, but he was refreshed from those few minutes. He ran everything through his mind again. He was satisfied he could do this thing. It would hurt like hell, but it needed to be done.

He brought out the water bottle and took a short swallow. Then he said, "What's the matter with me? Boy, am I dumb. I have another candy bar in my map case. I totally forgot it." He turned and looked in the back seat, where he had thrown his maps. Sure enough, there was the candy bar on the floor.

He picked it up and ripped the covering with his teeth and bit into it. He took some time to finish the bar and looked into the back seat to see if there was another one. He thought he had put three of them in before he left Chicago. He didn't see one. "Well, the one I found was chocolate. That should give me a little energy." He was on a roll, now. "Let's get this thing started," he said.

He put the bottle of water and topcoat back into the map case. He slowly reached over and tried the door. It opened with no problem. He put his map case out on what was left of the right wing. He raised the control yoke to a vertical position and began to inch his way toward the opening. It was extremely painful but after five minutes he had reached the opening.

He twisted around as best he could to look at his chances of getting the luggage compartment door to open. The wing stub was very rough, with torn and twisted aluminum slivers sticking up. He would have to be very careful sliding down. There was a small tree broken off in front of the luggage door, but he thought there might be room to get it open.

Scotty looked back across the clearing. The fog was getting very wispy at ground level. That would mean an air search could be started soon. The exertion had caused him to start bleeding again but that wasn't going to stop him now. He reached into the back and retrieved the first aid kit. He might need it after the trip down to the ground.

As an afterthought, he tried the radio one more time. He didn't get an answer. "Well, let's get started. Waiting isn't going to get me there." After that little pep talk and using only his good right arm, he inched his way out of the plane and onto the wing stub.

Bringing his broken legs out the door was extremely painful. Tears flowed down his cheeks and his vision blurred. He could hear and feel the broken bone ends rubbing against each other. It was sickening.

Mumbling, he forced himself backwards with a mighty thrust of his arm. He let out a scream that silenced the birds. He rolled a little to his right and retched. He brought up a green mess tinged with pink. The color of what came out didn't register in his mind at all. All he knew was he was out of the cockpit.

As he slid down the wing stub on his butt, he tried to bend down the aluminum slivers so they wouldn't open another wound or catch on his clothes. He inched his way backwards down to the trailing edge of the wing. He stopped several times to rest. Now he could feel a searing, fiery pain in his stomach.

Even though it was January the temperatures were warm. Mid thirties wasn't that bad. However, Scotty was soaked in perspiration and he was getting very cold. The weak January sun was finally making some progress burning off the fog. Now he could see all the way across the clearing and he could make out the path the Bonanza had taken. It made him shudder.

"I've got to get to those winter clothes. I'm freezing sitting here." He continued to make his way to the ground and his final destination, the luggage compartment door. Every time he moved forward, he flinched with pain. His arm, stomach, and legs were screaming for him to quit. All he could think of was warm clothes and not having to move again. He wanted to be warm again and just sleep for a few minutes.

Carefully, an inch at a time, he continued to slide down to the trailing edge of the wing. From the wing to the ground was a six-inch drop. *Very doable*, he thought. When his butt slipped over the edge and dropped to the ground, he lost his balance and fell, crushing his broken arm against the fuselage. A sharp pain shot through his whole body and brought tears to his eyes. He very carefully reached across his body with his right arm and pushed himself erect. He closed his eyes and let the pain subside. When it did, he continued to slide on his butt across the snow-covered ground until his legs were free of the wing.

"About another three feet," he told himself. He twisted his body until he had access to the luggage compartment door. He reached up and opened the door. It moved only a few inches and stopped at the tree stump, overlapping the tree by one-half inch. He didn't have enough strength left to force the door past the stump.

He opened the map case he had been pushing ahead of him, and took out his topcoat and spread it over his worn out body. He rested his back against the convenient tree stump as best he could and closed his eyes, but he didn't sleep. His mind was working as his body was resting.

Ten minutes later, he began to reposition himself. He took a good look at the tree stump. It was only two-inches thick. Maybe he could force the door past it. He just needed half an inch to get the door open.

He found a rock within reach. Using it as a hammer, he began hitting the center of the aluminum door until it began buckling. The more it bent, the harder Scotty hit it until finally it popped past the tree stump.

It had taken over an hour for Scotty to get to this point and he was tired and the pain that racked his body wasn't helping. He repositioned himself again so his back was leaning against the offending tree stump. He relaxed and closed his eyes.

That candy bar was still providing energy, and within ten minutes he was back at work. He reached into the luggage compartment and dragged out his winter coat. With a great deal of pain, he worked his good arm into the sleeve of the coat and then pulled the coat around his back and over his left shoulder. He managed to close the coat with two buttons. Within minutes he could feel the warmth coming back to his upper body.

After a short rest, he reached into the compartment and retrieved the sleeping bag and a small cardboard box. He unrolled the sleeping bag and wrapped it around his legs as best he could.

Next, he pulled the box to the edge of the opening. He opened the top and began pulling things out. Another bottle of water, and it wasn't frozen, a small sack of dried fruit, the flare pistol in its padded case, a box of flares, and a paper bag with several candy bars. Scotty was now convinced he had at least a chance to make it.

He pulled the map case closer and tipped it on its side. He retrieved his original bottle of water and took a great gulp. He tore the wrapper off another candy bar and began eating it. For the first time since this ordeal started, somewhere over Wisconsin when he realized he had a solid undercast of thick heavy fog, he let a smile creep across his face.

CHAPTER FOURTEEN

FRIDAY AFTERNOON GRACE CAME INTO SCOTTY'S OFFICE and asked, "How would you like to take me out for a nice quiet dinner tonight?"

"I'd love to. Do you have a taste for something special or somewhere you would like to go?"

"Somewhere it's quiet. Somewhere we can talk and enjoy ourselves. No, I don't want to take the plane to some exotic restaurant miles from here. Just somewhere we can be ourselves and relax."

"I have just the spot in mind. It'll meet all your requirements. I'll give them a call and reserve a table. Do you want to leave from here or go home to freshen up a little?"

"It's been a hard week for both of us and I'm tired. Let's leave from here so we won't get home so late, "Grace answered.

At 5:00 Grace and Scotty locked up the hanger and headed for a small oriental restaurant off the beaten path. It was indeed quiet. They were the only early diners. One of the waitresses seated them in a private room just off the main dining room. After the waitress left with their wine order, Grace commented, "Now this is quiet, very private, and we get to sit on the cushioned floor. How do you rate this kind of treatment?"

"I've been coming here by myself for a long time. I knew they had these private tearooms so I asked if we could have our dinner in one of them. Mostly these rooms are reserved for the owner's family. Do you like it?"

"Scotty, you always have the right answer to a maiden's prayer right at your fingertips. I love it."

The waitress came back with the wine and took their food order. After she left the room, Grace asked, "Scotty, we haven't talked about what you want out of our marriage. I think it's about time we both speak freely about our expectations. With that said, what do you see us doing in the next, let's say, five years?"

Grace had not looked at Scotty during her explanation and question. Now she looked up and saw a beaming smile on Scotty's face. "I thought there was something bothering you when you asked for a nice quiet dinner.

"To answer your question . . . in five years, I'd like to see a nice home on a large plot of land, possibly a small to medium-sized farm, with a little grass strip and a hanger for my toys. At least two children and a bank account large enough for us to be comfortable and to send our kids to college. I have ideas about ten years too, but let's first get through the first five. Now it's your turn."

Grace took a long time to respond. She had been leaning forward on the table, her arms on both sides of her wine glass and her hands folded. She looked into Scotty's eyes and, in an off-handed manner, commented, "Daddy, I'm sure glad you said those wonderful things. Maybe we should start looking for that farm."

At first Scotty thought her calling him Daddy was cute. His mom and dad sometimes did that. Then the smile fell from Scotty's face and his jaw dropped open as Grace's words sank in. "Wait a minute. Are you telling me you're pregnant?"

"Yes, sweetheart, I am. At least that's what the doctor told me this morning."

Scotty's head was exploding. "We'll have to tell the family and I'll have to let Ben know. How long will you be able to work? We'll have to get a temporary person to cover for you." Scotty ran on for a few more sentences and then began laughing. "Listen to me. I sound like, I don't know, kind of like I'm scared or something."

Grace had her arms around her stomach she was laughing so hard. About then, the waitress appeared with their dinner. The two of them calmed down and settled in to eat.

When they had finished and both had a cup of tea in front of them, Scotty asked, "How far along are you?"

"The doctor thinks about two months. So we have time to get things ready and maybe we should start looking for a farm somewhere close to an airport or build one on the farm."

"Maybe we should. Well, should we go home now, mama-to-be?"

"I'm ready, papa-to-be."

On the ride home, Scotty's mind was racing. Who should they tell first? Where should they look for a permanent home? What would Ben's response be? Questions that seemed completely ridiculous rumbled around his head. *Kim, that's whom he should call first.* He turned to look at Grace sitting next to him. "I can't remember, have I told you how much I love you lately?"

"Not for the last thirty minutes at least, and I'm feeling a little neglected. Tell me what you're feelings are right now."

Scotty took a few minutes to collect his thoughts, when he was ready he placed his right hand over hers and slowly began talking. "First and I guess, foremost, I'm very happy. Next, I'm confused. I'm not sure what we should do first. I know my love for you hasn't changed, but now I feel a lot more protective. I know we should tell the grandparents-to-be, but I think we should tell Kim first."

"I hate to tell you this, my darling, but Kim already knows. I called her right after I got back from the doctor's office. Her first words were, 'It's about time you two joined the crowd.'"

"That sounds like my little sister."

After arriving home, Scotty sat down on the sofa with a pad of paper and a pen. Grace sat next to him, and they began planning their new home and brainstorming what they wanted by the way of land and location. Somewhere around midnight, when they had talked it out and had it all down on paper, they turned in for the night. As they lay in each other arms, they kissed and slowly, melding into each other, made love.

Just as Scotty and Grace unlocked their office, the telephone began ringing. Grace answered it and then said, "Hi, Ben. Yes, Scotty's here. Just a minute. I'll get him on the line." She touched the hold button, turned to Scotty and commented, "A very excited Ben is on the line for you."

Scotty picked up the phone, "Morning, Ben. How's things in Chicago?"

"Scotty, I need you to pack your suitcase, grab your passport and be on the afternoon flight to Tunis. I bought an old, converted, B24. I took the word of an old Army Air Force buddy of mine that the plane is in good shape and capable of flying back to the states.

"He flew it during World War II and bought it from the government at the end of the war. He started a small airfreight company and did very well. Three of the four engines were just overhauled, and the fourth needs to be done but he believes it will make the trip back to the states without a problem.

"You are the only pilot in the company, besides me, that has time in the B24. I'd like you to pick it up and fly to London's Heathrow airport. I'll meet you there. We'll refuel and fly it back to Chicago. It shouldn't take more than three or four days. We do have a time constraint because the license expires in ten days and I'll need the plane here in Chicago to do a major on the fourth engine. Scotty listened to this one-sided conversation and looked over at Grace and mouthed, "You were right."

After Ben hung up, the phone rang almost immediately. It was Ben again. "Scotty, I forgot to tell you, the man who will meet you at the airport is Gene Andrews. I flew with him as co-pilot several times during the war. He's a great guy. Tell him I still love him." And he hung up.

That afternoon, Grace delivered Scotty and his luggage to the airport where he boarded the TWA flight to Tunis. Late the next evening he deplaned at Tunis-Carthage airport, went through customs with no problems and found Gene Andrews waiting for him in the customs office. *Interesting*, he thought.

After customs finished with Scotty's luggage, Gene picked up Scotty's flight bag. Scotty took his map case and followed Gene out of the building.

"How come you're selling this plane? I should think it would be something you would want to keep, if for no other reason than the memories."

"It's because of those memories that I need to sell it," Gene commented. The French Government has been trying to take over my company during the past two years. We did some flying for the locals and a few trips importing products for their use. Stuff the French didn't want in their hands. Then, finally the French gave Tunisia its independence in March of 1956. The new government was so happy with me they granted me another 5,000 hectares of ground. Now with 10,000 hectares we were able to improve the airfield to be able to handle larger aircraft.

"This is a long way from an old German fighter strip. This is better than a lot of commercial airports in the states. It's certainly the best private strip I've ever seen," Scotty exclaimed in an awed voice.

"Over the past few years, it's taken on a life of its own. All I have to do now is sit back and watch it grow. Well, here's the hanger where we keep the old Liberator. Do you want to take a look at her now?"

"I'm tired, Gene. But I'd like to look her over quickly. Then I'd like to go through her log books, and I'm sure there are more than one, plus all of the maintenance forms. That should keep me busy for a day of two. Then I'd like to go over her with a fine toothcomb inside and out. After that, I'd like a few hours flying time to get used to her before leaving. I need to call Ben before I leave, too. He wants to know when I'll get to Heathrow."

"I have all the paperwork in an office in the hanger. You can work there and I've got a Jeep you can use to get you back to the house."

He pulled up and parked close to a side door in the hanger. Inside, Scotty got a look at the old Liberator, squatting right in the center of the hanger. From where he stood, she looked to be in top shape. Very different from the usual used aircraft he picked up.

He walked, slowly, all the way around the plane. It had a unique paint scheme and the paint was the only thing he could find that showed age, and that was just a little fading. Gene had pushed a metal stairway in front of the cabin door and opened it.

Scotty entered the cabin and walked up to the cockpit. A quick glance showed him a completely equipped flight deck, including all of the latest electronic navigation equipment along with weather radar.

Something they had just begun putting on commercial planes in the States. *Whoever gets this plane won't have to do anything except repaint.* He turned to Gene and commented, "She sure looks to be in good shape. Show me to the office. All of a sudden, I'm not tired anymore. I need to learn more about this old girl."

Two days later Scotty was ready to fly the Liberator. He had looked over the service notes on the fourth engine and couldn't find anything out of the ordinary.

The following morning, Scotty and Gene took the B24 back into its primary element. They flew to several other airports totally on instruments. Scotty was surprised at how easy it was to fly, and said as much to Gene.

"One of the reasons she handles so well is there are no gun blisters hanging out in the slip stream. All of the armor plate has been removed. In fact, all of the equipment that makes it a warplane has been removed.

"She'll fly faster at full load now than we could empty in the old days. All that and she handles like a dream at slow approach speeds even in a crosswind. It's been a real joy to fly." The nostalgia in Gene's voice was hard to miss.

Scotty called Grace late that afternoon hoping she would be at the hanger. She was. He told her he would be leaving early the next morning and would meet Ben in England. They would probably leave England the following morning and he should be in town late the day after.

Next, he called Ben. Ben said, "Tell you what, Scotty. I'm going to be leaving late today. We'll be taking the Lear or the Citation, so I should be at our agent's hanger when you get there." And he hung up."

Scotty spent a quiet evening with Gene and his family. After supper he went to his bedroom and got everything ready for the following morning.

He awoke before dawn and quietly went down to the Jeep and drove to the airfield. He loaded his gear into the plane and with the sun peeking over the horizon he began a slow outside inspection of the aircraft. He hated surprises. He would be flying this big four-engine aircraft all by himself to England and he wanted to enjoy the flight.

At full light, Gene came into the hanger. "I heard you leave this morning. It's going to be a long lonely flight."

"I just couldn't sleep anymore. With your help and some change, I can get a couple candy bars and some soft drinks out of the vending machine. That'll hold me over until I get to Heathrow. Then I can con Ben into buying dinner."

Gene laughed, "Sounds just like me when I was your age. Come on let's get this bird out of its nest."

Gene attached the tow bar to the nose wheel while Scotty backed the tug into place. Slowly, he towed the big Liberator out of the hanger onto the concrete ramp. Gene put chocks under the wheels.

Gene came striding back to the plane. As he approached, he extended his hand "It was good to meet you, and I know we'll be doing more business together in the near future. The boys in the tower are aware of your flight. Give them a call, and they'll get you started. Have a good flight, and have Ben give me a call when you get back to the States."

"I want to thank you and your family for making me feel at home. The food was great and your wife is a real charmer. I know we'll be back."

Scotty moved quickly into the pilot seat and began the engine starting sequence. One at a time the four engines growled to life. Scotty watched the engine instruments as they warmed up. He picked up the microphone and called the tower. They gave him directions to the active runway. He waved to Gene, and Gene waved back. He advanced the throttles and moved away toward the active runway. Ten minutes later he was rocketing down the runway and into the air.

The tower crew had activated his flight plan. He began a climbing turn to reach his cruising altitude and compass heading. He set the auto pilot and sat back to enjoy the trip.

Chapter Fifteen

THE ARRIVAL AT HEATHROW was on Scotty's time estimate. The old Liberator performed like a perfect lady. Ben met the plane as it pulled into its parking place. He had three people and a dog with him. They were the customs people with a drug-sniffing dog. They quickly went through the cabin, cockpit, and baggage area. They completed their inspection in less than five minutes, stamped Ben's paperwork and left.

The fuel truck pulled up and refueling began. Scotty checked the engine oil on all four engines. Number four was low, but not as bad as he had expected. He brought the level up to maximum and did another walk around. When the refueling was completed, he checked the levels in all tanks and closed the filler caps.

Scotty walked into the line office where Ben was poring over maps and weather reports. "Scotty, how do you feel? We have some weather problems coming up over the North Atlantic if we wait too long. Can you handle leaving now?"

"Let's take a look at what you have." Scotty looked at the twenty-four-hour weather reports and commented, "I see what you mean. I don't see any reason why we couldn't leave right away. I can get us started and you can take over minding the baby while I take a short nap. Besides, Gene told me you were a pretty good B24 pilot yourself. So, I see no reason why we can't share the controls during the crossing.

"The auto pilot works very well and we have weather avoidance radar. We also have a few perks you guys didn't have when this baby was a bomber. We have an on-board bathroom, no relief tubes. We have a big plus in our extended range. Remember, Gene doubled the effective range by installing larger fuel tanks. We could fly to Chicago if we had to.

"As long as you're the copilot, you file a great circle flight plan to Boston's Logan Airport. We'll have to be careful of that fourth engine.

It's burning a lot of oil. We may have to shut it down for a period of time. We can do that as long as the other three continue to run.

"I've checked the engine oil in all four and we've been refueled, so as far as I'm concerned, we can leave as soon as you get our flight plan filed and I get us some sandwiches and coffee."

Twenty minutes later, Scotty was taxiing out to the active runway with Ben occupying the right seat. They received their clearance as soon as they finished their pre-flight checks. Scotty advanced all four of the throttles to full take-off power. Ben called out the speed, and Scotty lifted the big Liberator off the ground and called out, "Retract landing gear and flaps."

Scotty continued to climb to his assigned cruising altitude, settled on coarse and switched on the autopilot. He missed not having music in the cockpit. It always made the trip a little something special.

After about thirty minutes, Scotty checked their ground speed. "It looks like we have a light tail wind. We can make a better economy cruising speed than this old bird's top speed in military configuration. We're making three hundred twenty miles-per-hour ground speed."

"A great start to a memorable trip," Ben commented.

Scotty opened a candy bar and took a cup of water. When he had finished he disconnected the autopilot, slowly, throttled back the fourth engine, shut off the fuel, and feathered the propeller. He made slight adjustments to the control trim tabs until they could fly straight and level on the three engines and re-engaged the autopilot.

He watched the instruments very carefully. Air speed had dropped only five miles-per-hour. Ben dialed in the frequency of the navigation beacon ship anchored in the Atlantic. They were still on course. Scotty was satisfied. "Ben, it's getting dark and I'm tired. I'm going in the back and lie down for a nap. If anything changes, call me right away. In any event, call me in an hour."

An hour later, Scotty came back to the flight deck. "You didn't sleep very long. Are you sure you're rested enough?" Ben asked.

"Sure, I'm well rested. It doesn't take me long to come back. Why don't you go back and take a little nap yourself?"

"I think I will. I'd like to be up here to see us make landfall."

Scotty checked his navigation. He did the math twice to make sure of his numbers. Sure enough they were behind schedule. He put on his earphones and cut out the cockpit speakers so the radio wouldn't bother Ben. Then he placed a call to the beacon ship for a weather update. The predicted weather problem for the crossing was moving faster then the weather people had predicted. With this new information, he requested and got a change in altitude to a more favorable wind speed. They still had a head wind but now it was only fifteen miles per hour. They were coming up on their point of no return. That point where it would be closer to continue their trip then to turn back. He checked fuel consumption. They had plenty of fuel to get to Boston.

When they were an hour away from making landfall, Scotty woke Ben. "Boy, did I sleep. How's the coffee supply?"

Scotty answered, "The coffee's right behind your seat. There's a bag of sandwiches alongside the coffee. While you're pouring, fill my cup and give me one of the sandwiches."

"So, let's see if we can bring number four back on line."

Scotty opened the fuel line to number four, primed it and worked the starter switch. The propeller began to turn and soon the engine instruments began to register life. Scotty advanced the throttle and changed the propeller pitch to cruise configuration. He made slight changes in the engine controls and then said, "Ben, take the controls and turn off the auto pilot. I'll adjust the trim so the auto pilot won't have to work so hard and we won't be surprised later."

Ben did as he was asked and Scotty trimmed the plane to straight and level then re-engaged the autopilot. About that same time Ben spoke in a sharp voice, "Scotty, fire warning light in number four."

Scotty's eyes flew to the instrument panel, took in the flashing red light and scanned the other instruments. He shut off the fuel to number four, pulled the throttle back and feathered the prop. He grabbed the controls and said, "My airplane, Ben." Ben's hands and feet came away from the controls and he looked at Scotty.

Scotty pushed forward on the controls even before Ben's hands were clear. He put the plane in a steep diving turn with the number four engine on the high side trying to blow the fire out with the air rushing through the engine cowling. It worked.

Slowly, Scotty brought the Liberator back on course and regained the lost altitude. When they had both relaxed, Scotty said, "My, that never happened before. We'll let the engine cool off for a few minutes and try again. Maybe I primed it a little too much. We'll see how it works in a few minutes.

"You really move fast. But why didn't you pull the fire bottle?" Ben asked.

"We wouldn't have been able to start the engine again until it had been disassembled and cleaned out. That would have cost you money and a lot of lost time. If I could blow it out, we could try starting it again and we wouldn't have to inform Boston we were coming in on three engines.

"Well, let's try it again. Take the controls, Ben. I'll see if we'll have a running fourth engine."

Scotty carefully began the engine start sequence a second time. This time he didn't prime the engine quite so long. The propeller made about four rotations and the engine caught. He watched it through the co-pilot's window. No fire. "Well, we seem to have four engines running now. I'll get inbound clearance for us." He contacted the inbound controller and was given landing instructions. Their Atlantic crossing was coming to an end.

"Scotty, take the controls. I'm too nervous. I'm glad it was you that had the smarts to blow out that fire. I would have pulled the fire bottle and declared an emergency."

Scotty completed the landing at Logan field and created quite a stir at the refueling area with the Liberator. As soon as they were refueled and Scotty had checked the oil level in all four engines, they were on their way to Chicago. Scotty turned the controls over to Ben as soon as they had reached their cruising altitude.

"By the way, Ben, just before you called to send me on this trip, Grace told me we were going to be parents. She'll have to be replaced, at least temporarily, within the next four or five months."

"Scotty, that's great news. I'm happy for you both. I suppose I'm in the dog house with Grace because of this trip."

"No, not at all. Grace knows I have to be gone for these special projects. I don't think it's a problem yet, but it will be in a few months. All right, Ben. It's time you took over the pilot's chair. I'll be your copilot for the last landing."

Ben looked at Scotty and without a word, moved to the left seat. The landing was perfect, and Scotty said, "See, I said you could do it and you did. Nice soft landing. Just the kind of landing I would expect out of a good bomber pilot."

Both men slid their side windows open to get some fresh air into the cockpit. The ramp in front of Aircraft Unlimited was crowded with people watching the boss bring in the Liberator.

The line chief rolled a stairway over to the cabin cargo door. Ben had opened only one side of the double doors and the line chief came running up the stairs, "How was the trip? Did you have any problems?"

Ben looked over at Scotty, who made an insignificant shake of his head. "No problems at all," Ben answered. "It was a long, boring, flight. Scotty and I shared the piloting duties, and we both had an opportunity to get some sleep. However, I'm very tired now and I know Scotty wants to call Grace to let her know that we're back. And, speaking of Grace, Scotty told me that she's pregnant. If I understand correctly, she'll be taking a short leave of absence in a few months. If any of you talk to her, make sure she knows how we all feel."

Scotty and Ben walked across the flight line and into Ben's office. Ben checked his mail and found a letter he had been waiting for. "Scotty, this is what I've been waiting for. It's going to be your next project. I found a World War I Sopwith Camel on a ranch in Australia. The rancher has been using it to keep track of his cattle. We've had several conversations over the past few months. He's finally agreed to sell it to me.

"In a week or so, I'd like you to fly down there to disassemble and crate the plane for shipment back to your place. You did such a nice job with your Bonanza, I'd like you to restore the Sopwith. Besides, you're going to need something to keep you busy until your baby gets here. After the Australia trip, I promise, I won't send you on long trips for at least a year.

"Now go home. Take a week off. I'll have your airline tickets and export paperwork ready to go by next week. Take the time to relax and take Grace somewhere nice for dinner on the company. Then you can tell her about this next trip. She'll be mad at me for a while but I think she'll understand."

Grace picked Scotty up at the airport early in the evening. "Have you had supper yet, Grace?"

"No not yet. I thought I'd wait until you got back. I need to hear all about this trip. It sure didn't take you as long as I thought it would. Are you up to going out to eat, or are you too tired?" Grace asked.

"Well, the boss instructed me to take you out to a nice place for dinner. On the company I might add. To answer your question, Yes, I'm tired but I'm also hungry. Besides, I like to be seen in the company of beautiful women, especially those who are pregnant with my child."

"Okay, Scotty, what does Ben want this time?"

"I'll make you a deal. Let's find a place to eat and relax a little. Then, I'll give you the whole story, I promise."

Without a word, Grace took an off ramp and then a right turn into the parking lot of a restaurant specializing in steak. "As long as Ben is paying, let's enjoy the best. We haven't had a prime rib since you took me to New York for dinner and then seduced me. Do you suppose that could happen again even if we aren't in New York?"

Scotty leered at Grace and commented in an off-handed manner, "Well, if you play your cards right, it, just, might."

After ordering a cocktail and the steaks, Grace folded her hands around her glass and asked, "Do I have to wait until the meal is over to find out why I'm being bribed?"

Scotty chuckled, "No, young lady, you don't have to wait. Ben's found a World War I Sopwith Camel in flying condition down in Australia and he wants me to go down there, disassemble it and bring it back here to Minneapolis." Grace's face lost its smile, her eyes began flashing and she took a big breath in preparation for an outburst. Scotty held up both of his hands and continued, "Before you blow up, hear me out. Let me finish Ben's reasoning.

"On the flight back, I told him about our being pregnant and that we would have to find a replacement for you. Not a permanent replacement, but at least a temporary one. I also told him that when the baby gets here, I'd like some time away from the flying part of the business and more time here at home.

"He agreed to my request with the condition that I do this one last long trip for him. He also wants me to restore the Sopwith to flyable condition here in our hanger. I'm going to ask him to send up one of the Chicago people to mind the office while you and I go to Australia together. We haven't had a real vacation since our honeymoon. The Sopwith will be shipped back by boat and then by truck from the West Coast. That'll take at least three to four weeks."

Grace sat with her head down and her hands gripping her glass. She was silent for a few minutes, twisting the glass first one way then the other. Finally, she looked up and Scotty could see a tear working its way down her cheek. "Did you really mean that? Did he really agree to take you off flying status and will you really ask him to let me go?"

Scotty put his hands over Grace's and, gently, squeezed. "Yes, I meant it. Yes, Ben agreed and, yes, I'm going to call him first thing in the morning."

"Scotty, I've always worried about you when you're flying some of these old planes he has you chasing after. This last flight absolutely terrified me. All I could see was you falling into the ocean in that old bomber, and our baby growing up not knowing his father. I didn't like that feeling a bit."

"Oh, come on, Grace. You know me better then that. You know I don't take chances. You know I check out these airplanes before I fly any of them anywhere. That old Liberator is in great shape. It never missed a beat." Scotty didn't like telling her that, knowing it was a small lie. But in her present condition he couldn't tell her about the number four engine catching fire. She just wouldn't understand. Anyway, as far as he was concerned, he and Ben were never in any danger. That was the important part.

CHAPTER SIXTEEN

S COTTY BEGAN TO MOAN AND MOVE HIS HEAD from side to side. His upper body began trembling and, with a quick intake of breath, his eyes popped open. Terror washed over him but slowly faded as his mind caught up to the fact that he was out of the plane and his body registered severe pain everywhere.

"I need to be careful," he told himself aloud. "I must have passed out. I need to stay awake. I might miss a passing airplane, or I could freeze to death."

A movement out in the woods caught his attention. A look of pleasure crossed his face and he perked-up with a little enthusiasm. "Look at that. My little deer friend came back. It's nice to see another living creature. Oh, now the pain is really coming back. Legs are hurting, head is pounding." At that moment a violent tremor passed through his body.

Even with the winter coat and sleeping bag over him, he could still feel the cold. "Maybe I should try the emergency radio while I can. Don't know how long the battery will hold up." Scotty could see that the sun was getting lower on the horizon. It was good to see that sun after so much fog.

He'd save the flares for after dark. They could be seen from a long way off. When he moved, he could tell his stomach was bloated and the pain was worse now. He feared it was internal bleeding. Not good. He turned the power switch on the emergency radio, twisted the frequency dial and tried, "Mayday, Mayday Bonanza one victor. Can anyone hear me?" No response. Nothing.

"Doesn't look like anyone can hear me. Wonder how long I've been here. Feels like at least a day. Pain is—getting bad. So tired."

Scotty's eyes closed again and his head dropped to his chest. The microphone slipped from his hand and came to rest in his lap. The radio speaker crackled at a very low volume and a voice came through, barely audibly, "Alix flight service, this is Piper Arrow six six niner Charlie. I can hear a Mayday message on your frequency."

"Niner Charlie we are aware of it. We have search parties out looking for him. Thanks for the information though. What's your position?"

"We're about twenty miles due south of the field. We tried to get a fix on him but his carrier went off too fast."

"Roger, niner Charlie. Thanks for the information."

The radio worked, but Scotty didn't hear it.

CHAPTER SEVENTEEN

THE NEXT MORNING AFTER GETTING HOME from picking up the Liberator, Scotty called Ben and asked him to send up an office person to mind the store while he and Grace flew to Australia. Ben agreed. Within two weeks they were on their way. The owner of the Sopwith, Willard Cathcart, picked them up at the Sydney airport in a twin Beechcraft and flew them back to his ranch.

Scotty looked out of the side window at the ground passing under the plane. He estimated they were flying about 3,500-feet above the ground. He watched the countryside go from a lush green and obviously a concentrated human population to a dry countryside with rocky outcroppings, flat sandy soil, a scattering of vegetation here and there. It looked somewhat like the southwestern United States.

"Is this what you call the Outback?" Scotty asked Willard.

"Yes, it is. We've been flying over my ranch for the past fifteen minutes. We'll have another thirty minutes to go to reach my airfield. It's a good two hours flying time to Sydney in this plane. With the Sopwith it would take about five or more hours with at least three gas stops."

"I don't think I want to fly the Sopwith into Sydney airport anyway," Scotty said. "A busy airport like that, I don't think the tower people would be very happy about an old slow biplane wanting to land there even at a slow time of the day.

"I think what we'll do is remove the wings and engine, then truck it back to Sydney. I've already talked to the freight forwarder there, and they'd prefer to build the shipping container. That way the insurance won't be as costly. However, I do want to fly it before we begin the shipping preparations," Scotty commented.

"We'll try to get you in the air yet today. The ground training will take just a few minutes. The airplane just about flies itself. Top speed is only somewhere in the 125 kilometer range. There is no air speed instrument, just a piece of cloth tied to the wing strut. But we'll fill you in shortly. There's my airfield just a few miles ahead."

Forty-five minutes later, the Beechcraft had been refueled and tucked away in its private hanger. Willard took Scotty and Grace into a larger hanger right next to the Beechcraft's. Scotty came through the door right after Grace. He came to a dead stop just three steps into the building.

"Will you look at that," he exclaimed. "I can't believe this air force you've got."

Grace took a long slow look at the stagger-wing Beech. "It's beautiful," she exclaimed.

"And, look over in the corner, that's the Sopwith. There's an S.E. 5, and it looks like it's ready to go on patrol over the front lines. Willard, is that an American Standard in the back corner?"

"Yes, it is, Scotty. And you're right, all of them are flyable and the S.E. 5 is really a later version. It's an S.E. 5a. It has a 206 horsepower Hispano Suiza engine with a four-blade propeller that gives it more speed and more maneuverability. The only plane I have that's not ready to fly is an original Fokker Dr1 Tri-plane. It's over in my workshop. If your boss has some other collectors that would like one of these, they're all for sale. Including the Tri-plane I just told you about. My wife tells me I need to cut down my personal air force as she calls it."

"We'll give Ben a call later. Maybe he has some friends who would like one of them. As long as I'm here, we might as well do what we can. Look at that Beechcraft. Take a look inside. It's not as fast as our Bonanza but it sure is pretty. Climb into the passenger seat and feel how comfortable it is."

Scotty helped Grace into the plane and she settled in. "Yes, it is very comfortable and I must admit it's easier to get into. It even has that new car smell."

Willard said, "We just finished this one. I got the air-worthiness certificate just this past week. Let's get you both settled into your room. I'm sure you'd like to freshen up a bit, and the misses will want to meet you both. After that, if you want to take the Sopwith for a spin, Scotty, we'll get you checked out."

Over the next two days, Scotty flew the Sopwith three times for a total of two and a half hours. The following day they called Ben to see if he wanted any of the other planes. Ben thought for a few minutes and told Scotty, "I'll have to make a few calls but I think I have a friend who might like the S.E. 5a. I tell you what . . . I'll try to catch up with him tomorrow. And to avoid the problem of the time difference, I'll fax you at Willard's ranch."

Willard and Scotty began disassembling the Sopwith camel. By the time Ben's fax came, they had both upper and lower wings off with all parts numbered for reassembly. Ben wanted the S.E. 5a. Scotty flew it and announced it a great airplane. Over the next three weeks, Willard and Scotty prepared both planes for shipment back to the States.

Early on a Monday morning, two trucks with small flatbed trailers showed up at the ranch. With help from the ranch hands, they loaded the two planes onto the trailers, and the trucks began their journey to Sydney harbor.

Their work done, Scotty and Grace hopped a commercial airliner back to the United States. As soon as they were home, Grace began looking for that piece of farm property big enough to put in a landing strip and to build their new house. She found several sites south and west of town but close enough to commute by car or light plane.

A few weeks later they made an offer on an 160-acre farm just west of Jordan, Minnesota. It had a wonderful old two-story prairie home that Grace decided she wanted to renovate. The barn and outbuildings were in good shape, and Scotty felt the barn could be modified for use as a hanger for the Bonanza.

Their offer was accepted, and the day after the closing, a crew moved in to remodel the house under Grace's supervision. A second crew of workers came in and, under Scotty's direction, leveled out two crossing runways and replanted grass. A few months later, little William (Billy) MacTavish II was installed in his own room on the second floor, right next to his proud parents' room. The MacTavish Air Farm was open for visitors.

True to his word, Ben left it to Scotty alone to get both planes ready to be re-licensed by the FAA. Both planes were completed before the end of summer. Scotty flew the S.E. 5a to Chicago and the new owner picked it up the same day.

Ben came out of his office and called, "Scotty, I need to see you for a few minutes. When you get everything set up, come on in."

"I'll be right there, Ben, in maybe two or three minutes."

When Scotty walked into Ben's office, Ben popped out of his chair. "Scotty, you did a great job with both those old birds. The new owner of the S.E. 5a called to tell me that the plane handles like a dream. He's loaning it to the EAA (Experimental Aircraft Association) museum in Oshkosh, Wisconsin, for a few years. He said he'd fly it during the EAA fly-in next summer. Now, I want to show you what we've been doing with the old B24 Liberator."

They walked over to another hanger and Ben opened the service door. He turned on the lights, and Scotty caught his breath. There sat the Liberator in all its glory, sporting a new paint job in the company colors of white with bright blue trim and numbers. With AIRCRAFT UNLIMITED in large bright blue letters scrawled in script on the side of the fuselage.

"Come on, let's go inside. I want you to see the new company Executive Airliner." They climbed up the new air stair door that had been installed. Walking into the cabin was like walking into a living room of an executive's home. Everything was color coordinated, including the business office or cockpit. Full instrumentation and updated weather radar. It now had the latest and greatest of everything.

Scotty turned and looked at Ben with an impish grin on his face, "Do you think you might have gone a little overboard with this thing?"

The smile dropped from Ben's face, "Is it too glitzy?"

"No, Ben. It's really beautiful, but you must have spent a lot of money on this old airplane. Are you sure it'll earn its keep?"

"Scotty, you're talking like a finance manager or a banker. I'm working with a lot of corporate executives now. This is an advertisement, not only for the sales department but also for our service facility. Yes, I think it'll earn its keep. At least for a while."

"It is a beautiful renovation. Have you done anything to improve performance?"

"Actually, we have. We installed larger fuel tanks, and the whole plane is pressurized."

Scotty chuckled. "Ben, it looks like it's your personal toy."

Now Ben chuckled. "Well, maybe there's some of that, too. But you must admit it'll make a great addition to our fleet.

"Now, let's get back to business. I'm going to send you back home in the Lear. I want you to send Grace and little Billy back to Chicago in the Lear. Then, I want you to bring the Sopwith here tomorrow. We might even have the S.E. 5a back here. We're going to have a coming out party for the Liberator on Friday with a company open house. We've sent out invitations to all our customers and some potential customers.

"Plan on spending the weekend here. We have some business we need to take care of before you go home."

"All right Ben. I'll give Grace a call and give her some warning. When's the Lear leaving?"

"Anytime you're ready to leave. The pilot can stay overnight. He can leave tomorrow morning with Grace and Billy. My office people need to spend some time with Grace. We have some new office equipment she'll need and you'll be taking all of it back with you Monday morning."

Later, when Scotty walked out to the Lear, Don Kopinski came around the tail of the jet. "Your cab awaits you, oh mighty one," came the sarcastic remark from Scotty's best friend within the company.

"Ah, the ace pilot of the company is to take me back to my blushing bride. I can now feel completely safe. Lead on, my brother of the skies," came Scotty's equally sarcastic answer.

When Scotty arrived back in Minneapolis, Grace was waiting for him at the hanger. The three of them gassed the plane then moved it into an open space in the hanger.

"Grace, did you make a reservation for Don somewhere?"

"Yes. He has a late arrival guaranteed room at that little mo-tel motel just down the road. I'm sure he'll be able to find whatever he might want for his evening entertainment."

"Grace, that's really unkind. You know I'm a good kid and never do anything disreputable or out of the ordinary," Don said.

"One of these days, a cute little girl will grab you by the ears and lead you right up to an alter and you won't be able to say no. That's when your life will really change for the better," Grace commented.

"Amen." Scotty said with feeling.

"All right, you guys. I'm going to enjoy going out to dinner with two such handsome flyboys. Where would you like to take me?" Grace asked.

"I don't know about Scotty and you, Grace, but I'd like a big juicy rare steak."

"What would you like, Grace?" Scotty asked.

"Steak is good."

"Steak it is."

Later that evening, after taking Don to the motel, Grace said, "I've got some good news and some bad news. First, I'll give you the good news. Your teacher and mentor, Len Boerger, is going to retire. Now the bad news, Len has sold his planes and the business. The new owner will be taking over in two months. Len told your other teacher and mentor, Buster, that the new owner won't need a mechanic. So he'll be out of a job when the new owner takes over."

Scotty looked at Grace. "I'm happy for Len, but how is Buster going to find something else. He's a loner. He doesn't like a lot of people running around his shop. Maybe I can find something at our place. I have a suspicion that Ben's going to want us to do more renovation of older aircraft. Let me talk to Ben when we get to Chicago. If I can talk him into letting us get started on the renovation of tired old airplanes, Buster would fit right in."

The next morning dawned cloudy and dreary. A taxi pulled up to the front door of the hanger, and Don popped out of the back seat. And, true to his nature, he had a very pretty young lady in tow. "I promised her I'd take her to dinner and show her all the interesting places in town. You know Aircraft Unlimited, the libraries, museums, and my apartment."

Scotty and Grace welcomed her. Scotty commented, "Girl, I hope you know what you've let yourself in for." He turned to Don, "Have a good flight and take care. The weather's looking like it's going to be a wet flight for me. That's no big problem but it could set me back on my arrival time. I've equipped the Sopwith with a radio so I can get weather reports along the way. I'll be listening all the way down. When I get within range, I'll call on the company frequency."

Scotty watched Don, his new girl, Grace, and little Billy take off for Chicago. After the Lear disappeared into the clouds, Scotty put on his weatherproof flying clothes, started the engine and called the tower for clearance to taxi to the active runway. He did his preflight checks on the way to the runway. He received take off clearance as soon as he got to the end of the runway.

He advanced the throttle and the little Sopwith fairly jumped into the air. He activated his flight plan and continued his climb to a low twenty-five-hundred feet to stay under the clouds. He picked up Interstate 94 and put it on his right side and settled back to enjoy the flight.

The Sopwith performed well on the first leg of the journey. It wasn't a plane a pilot could trim up and fly hands off. There were no trim tabs, and it required one of his hands on the control stick at all times. He picked up a little tail wind so he made good time on this first leg.

He stopped in Wisconsin for fuel and rested long enough to enjoy a cup of hot coffee and a candy bar. Then he climbed back into the Sopwith and continued his trip. Scotty realized the clouds were lowering when he couldn't get above fifteen hundred feet without getting into clouds. Then the rain came. He put on his goggles to protect his eyes and took the Sopwith down a little lower so he could keep Interstate 94 in sight.

The rainfall increased and the winds began bouncing his little plane around. He tried going lower, but the rough air only got worse. He climbed back to just below the clouds and lowered his airspeed. That helped a little, but it was still a bumpy ride. The rain lasted about five minutes, then backed off to a drizzle but the convection currents in the air still gave him a rough ride.

When he was within twenty-five miles of the airport, Scotty called the company. "I should be at the hanger in thirty minutes or so. The heavy rain's stopped. Now it's mostly a heavy mist and very bumpy. Visibility is getting low. I hope the airfield won't close before I get there."

Ben's voice boomed in his headset, "Don't worry about the airfield. They know you're coming in, and they wouldn't dare close. As long as you have pattern altitude, you can sneak in under this stuff. We have a whole hanger full of people here waiting for you. Pull up to the main hanger when you get here. We've saved a place to bring the Sopwith in out of the rain. The S.E. 5a came in early this morning. Take care and we'll see you soon."

Scotty called the tower and got landing instructions and began a slow decent. He didn't have to go down very far to get to landing pattern altitude. On the downwind leg, he glanced at the front of the hanger and saw two people standing by the service door. As he watched, the big doors began opening.

Scotty's mouth dropped open and he commented to the wind, "Look at all the people. There must be at least a hundred there." Then as he turned onto the base leg, he could see a television remote truck behind the hanger. "Ben, what are you up to now?" he asked.

He turned his attention back to landing the Sopwith. Like all of its brothers, the Sopwith needed all his attention for a good landing. The wheels touched down, and he pinned it to the ground in a perfect two-point landing without a bounce. He kept the speed up coming down the runway until he approached the first turnoff. Then he pulled the throttle back to idle, let the tail drop and turned off the active runway and called ground control for clearance to the hanger.

As he pulled into the parking area in front of the hanger, he shut down the engine and coasted to a stop right in the center of the open hanger doors. He disengaged himself from the radio system, took off his helmet and climbed out of the plane. He could see the television cameras following his every move.

Ben walked toward him with a gigantic smile on his face. As he got close, he extended his hand to grasp Scotty's. Then he pulled him into a bear hug. Scotty pulled away and looked at Ben, "What did you get me into now, Ben? What are all these people and cameras doing?"

"All in due time, Scotty, all in due time. Right now, we want to push the Sopwith into the hanger. Then you'll get all the answers."

Six men came out of the crowd and turned the Sopwith around and rolled it into the hanger, tail first. When it was placed where Ben told them he wanted it, the big doors slid shut.

At the back of the hanger, a large area had been cleared and a small stage, about two feet high, had been erected. A podium was located in the middle of the stage complete with a microphone connection to the loud speakers in the hanger. As Ben and Scotty walked toward the stage, Ben leaned into Scotty's ear and said, "I want you up on the stage with me. I want you to stand just to my right. While I'm talking, I don't want any side comments out of you. You'll get your chance to talk after I'm through."

Ben walked to the podium and did what every speaker's always done. He tapped the microphone with his finger and then spoke into the microphone and asked, "Is this thing working?" Satisfied that it was working, he began, "Thank you all for coming out on this cold and wet day. This is a special day for all of us at Aircraft Unlimited. Most of you have had the opportunity to look at two of our latest projects, the S.E. 5a from World War One, the B24 Liberator from World War Two and now the Sopwith Camel that just landed, also from World War One. I'd like to give you a little background on all these old and well-respected birds.

"First is the Liberator. I tracked down the man I flew with during the Second World War. Those who know me know I flew Liberators out of North Africa. Well, he told me he had purchased his old Liberator from the government after the war, and he stayed in North Africa and started, what turned out to be, a very successful airfreight business. He continued to fly this plane until a few years ago. When he told me he wanted to sell it, I told him I wanted it. We agreed on a fair price and the deal was done. Now I had to get it back to the States. That's where this man on my right comes into the story.

"For those of you who don't know this man, let me introduce Brian MacTavish, better known in our flying circles as Scotty. By the way, for our friends in the press, I hope you all got the press package we prepared. It has background information on Scotty as well as our company. If you didn't get one, please see my secretary, Suzy, later. She'll be in the hanger office."

Ben turned a little and looked at Scotty. Ben thought he looked a little uncomfortable. "I have to tell you, folks. Scotty has no idea what I'm up to, so I'll get on with it. Scotty flew to North Africa and picked up the Liberator and flew it to London. I met him there, where we readied the plane for the flight back to the States. Scotty and I took turns flying that old bird across the Atlantic Ocean.

"When we landed in Boston, we were within three minutes of his estimated time of arrival, even though we were behind schedule at the half way point. And right on course all the way across. Let me tell you it was a thrill to fly that plane again. We brought it back here and began the renovation project. What you see is the result. And I can tell you it is now a very comfortable, easy to fly, corporate asset. It's also my personal transportation.

"Right after getting back, I found an advertisement in one of the flying magazines. A Sopwith Camel was for sale in Australia. I sent Scotty and his wife, Grace, down there to check it out. The same owner had the S.E. 5a for sale. Aircraft Unlimited bought both of them. Obviously Scotty is a great pilot but there was no way he was going to fly them both back from Australia, so he dismantled them both, had special crates built and moved them to the freight forwarding company. They ended up at our Minnesota facility and Scotty put both planes back together and got new airworthiness certificates for both of them.

"The S.E. 5a was sold to an individual who's going to exhibit his plane at the EAA museum in Oshkosh, Wisconsin. Right now I'm going to bring Scotty up to the mike and give him one of his two surprises." Ben pulled Scotty next to him and put his arm around his shoulders.

"You have been just a delight to me over the years, Scotty. You came to interview for a ferry pilot position several years ago, a brash young kid, full of confidence and ready to take on the world. You did just that. You became my 'go to' guy, like the sports commentators say or my good right hand. Never, once, did you question a project I gave you. Minneapolis was your idea and it has been a great challenge for you. And, I might add, you came through with flying colors. That office has developed a full one-third of Aircraft Unlimited income this year.

"So, on behalf of the company, I'd like to give you the title to the Sopwith Camel to add to your collection of great aircraft of history. It can sit right beside that beautiful V35 Beechcraft Bonanza of yours. That's your first surprise."

The crowd began to laugh, shout, whistle, and clap their hands all at the same time. Scotty stood there with a shocked expression on his face, looking at the title to the little Sopwith. He looked at Ben and just shook his head. Then a great big grin spread across his face and he thanked Ben.

Ben turned back to the microphone, "Now for the second surprise. Aircraft Unlimited has grown rapidly over the past three or four years, thanks to all our great people. It's time for me to get back to doing what I do best, marketing. Only now, I want to be doing it on a world scale.

"Much of our business has come from overseas and, as I see it, that will only increase in the future. With that thought in mind, I am going to promote Scotty to vice-president and general manager of Aircraft Unlimited with me as marketing manager, president, and CEO."

There was a roar of approval from the audience and a lot of applause. Ben continued, "Scotty will handle the day-to-day operations of both offices and will continue to operate out of Flying Cloud airport in Minneapolis as well as here in Chicago. I guess that's Eden Prairie instead of Minneapolis, isn't it Scotty?" Ben looked at Scotty and he nodded.

Ben then turned and looked out at the crowd of people in the hanger and commented, "Well, Mister Vice-President, is there anything you want to say?" Then he stepped back and pulled Scotty in front of the microphone.

Once again there was a roar of applause and cheers. Scotty looked completely dumbfounded. He looked around at the crowd in front of him and just shook his head in amazement. Finally everyone settled down except Scotty. "I don't know what to say. I didn't expect either of these surprises, as Ben called them. I was just doing my job like all the rest of you. I accept the Sopwith with the greatest of pleasure. It's a great little plane and a joy to fly.

"Now about the other thing the V.P. and general manager, I'm not sure I qualify, but I'll give it my best shot. And, along with my co-workers, we'll get the job done.

"Ben, come back here. I want to thank you from the bottom of my heart. This was totally unexpected. You know the Sopwith will have a good home. It's the other thing I'm not sure of, but thank you very much."

"Scotty, you've earned it." Ben looked out at the gathering and continued. "I'll be touring Europe and the Mid-East in a few weeks in that beautiful Liberator you've all been drooling over. I'll be renewing some old friendships, talking to some former customers and trying to drum up additional business. Scotty will be covering for me and running both locations from his Flying Cloud office.

"For our Aircraft Unlimited employees, we can't keep calling the company airliner, the Liberator. So, I'm offering a $500 check to the person that comes up with the best name in the `Name the Plane' contest. You have three weeks from today to think of a name. We'll need time to paint the name on the plane before I leave.

"I want to thank all of you for being here today. I'd like to give a special thanks to all of you in the flying press. This is the first live press release I've ever given. Please let the world know how dedicated we are to this industry. Thank you all. There's still some coffee, soft drinks, and goodies in the lounge."

A beaming Grace, little Billy, Scotty, and Ben left the makeshift stage and crossed the hanger floor to Ben's office.

When they were all seated in Ben's office, Scotty asked, "Do you know what you just did, Ben?"

"Oh, I think I do. I've put you in charge of a very successful business so I can go off in my personal toy as you called it. I know it's a shock to you at the moment, but you should have realized something was coming because I've been giving you so much authority to operate on your own.

"As I said at the press conference, the expansion was your idea, and now just a few years later it's producing a third of our total business. What are you going to do when you set up a service department? I'll bet the bottom line will emerge close to half of our total numbers. A service department is one of the projects I want you to tackle when you get back."

"I already have some ideas along that line, Ben. I'm sure you've heard by now that Len Boerger sold his flying service. The guy who taught me airframes and engines ran his shop. Buster is a great guy and he knows airplanes.

"The new owner of Len's flying service isn't going to continue a service facility. I'd like to hire Buster for our shop. He's a loner and sometimes a little hard to get along with, but he's as honest as they come and a very hard worker. If you have no objections, I'd like to bring him on board as soon as he's through at Len's."

"That's your call, Scotty. You're in charge in Minneapolis as well as here. From now on, I'm in charge of flying inventory, public relations, and sales. In a couple of weeks my wife and I will be leaving. I'm taking two of your young pilots with me so I don't have to do a lot of the flying. That's another problem you're going to have to address. We'll need at least three new pilots, preferably young so we can train them in our way of doing things."

"Okay, Ben. That's something I can do. My next question may throw you a little. Are we going to continue to renovate or restore older planes? If so, my idea is to use my facility for that type of work and this facility for major overhauls and heavy service work. I'd like to increase the size of our electronics service shop and center it here in Chicago, with a smaller sales and service shop in the Twin Cities."

"See, Grace, I am right," Ben said with a wink. "Already he's coming up with great ideas. Scotty, you go right ahead with all of that and if you come up with anything else, we'll talk about it. As president of this organization, I'd like to know what's going on, but you have a free hand with what we've discussed today.

"Grace, why don't you give Billy to my wife. She'll watch him for a while. You need to meet with my Suzy. She'll fill you in on the new equipment you'll be taking back with you, and she can fill you in on your additional responsibilities."

"By the way, Scotty, the Lear is now your personal company aircraft. You'll be taking that home. It's being loaded with the new office equipment and should be ready by the time we finish talking. You can come back at a later time to pick up your Sopwith. We'll keep it in the hanger here until you're ready to get it. Keep tonight open. We would like all three of you to have dinner with us. We'll need to spend some time together tomorrow before you head back."

CHAPTER EIGHTEEN

SCOTTY CAME BACK TO CONSCIOUSNESS WITH A COUGHING JAG. He coughed up a wad of blood and spit it to one side. Before he had a chance to look at it clearly, he regurgitated a large amount of blood that landed on his jacket and sleeping bag covering his legs.

"Looks like have some internal bleeding. If I survive this, Grace is gonna kill me." He paused and thought about that statement. Then he laughed at himself. "That was a really stupid remark." His mind became clear and some of his old strength returned. The laugh must have given him something to grab onto.

"I wonder if anyone has told her I'm overdue. How is she doing? How is Billy doing? I need to get out of here, now! I can see the headlines. Boy Genius dies in a plane crash. Pilot error and weather blamed." In a firm voice he shouted, "I WILL NOT DIE HERE!"

He picked up the microphone again and called for help. When he released the send button he realized the volume was turned down or the battery in the radio was low. No, that couldn't be. He had just put in a new battery a few weeks ago. He turned the volume up as high as it would go. Maybe if he fell asleep again a radio call might wake him.

After spitting up the blood, his stomach wasn't as queasy or as bloated. The arm and legs weren't as painful either. He wasn't sure if that was a plus or not. Maybe he was just getting used to the pain. He looked around the clearing and decided he would fire the first flare sometime in the next hour. By that time it would be dark.

What's that noise? It sounds like a plane somewhere to the northeast. He could just make it out. With hope running high now, he picked up the microphone again and called, "Mayday, Mayday this is Bonanza one victor. I hear your engine. You seem to be northeast of my location. Over."

He waited, nothing. No response. The air went out of his hopeful balloon and tears began running down his cheeks. He wept bitter tears for the next few minutes then collected his thoughts and wiped the tears away.

"Will I ever get out of here? Will I ever be found?" His voice cracked with frustration. He listened for the sound of the aircraft's engine. Nothing.

His body sagged and he closed his eyes to rest a little before he fired the first flare.

CHAPTER NINETEEN

B RIGHT AND EARLY SUNDAY MORNING SCOTTY, Grace, and little Billy were winging their way back home. "This leg of the trip is a lot quicker and a lot more comfortable than the trip down. A lot drier, too," Scotty commented.

"I'm sorry the Sopwith is a single cockpit. I'd like to take a spin in an open cockpit plane with you sometime," Grace said with a broad smile on her face.

"Well, maybe we'll get that chance sometime in the future. At least, I hope so. It's quite an experience, and in the winter, quite chilling."

"Are you going to try to land at the farm today," Grace asked.

"No, the Lear is too heavy for the farm strip this early in the season. The ground is still a little mushy. A few more landings and takeoffs will pack it down enough so we can use it. I'll bring the Sopwith back in a week or two and hanger it in the barn. I'll probably bring the Bonanza to the farm, too. We'll need all the hanger space we can get, at the field.

"I'm going to talk to the airport commission. I'd like to get at least one more large hanger with some out buildings or land to build at least two good-sized buildings. One of the new buildings for an engine shop the other for electronics and instrument service.

"I want to call Buster as soon as we get into the office. Do you know if the sale of Len's service went through?" Scotty asked.

"As far as I know, it's a done deal. I didn't get it from Len but from another pilot on the field. The new owner is supposed to take over the first of the month. I don't know if they had any service customers left after the sale announcement. Buster might be out already."

Scotty thought for a moment, "Let's try calling Len before we go to the farm. If Buster is already out of a job I'll ask Len for his home number. If they have some left over service obligations, maybe the new owner will let him finish the jobs. If not we'll see if we can move them to our hanger and Buster can complete the work there."

Grace picked up the microphone and called Flying Cloud for landing instructions.

"Lear three niner eight, cleared for straight in approach to runway two seven, right. Please show landing lights."

"Roger, twenty seven right straight in. Landing lights are on, and close our fight plan."

"Three, niner, eight, flight plan is closed. You did it again, Scotty. Your touchdown will be right on the minute. Contact ground control for taxi instructions."

"Roger. Thank you."

As Scotty turned off the active runway, Grace changed the radio frequency and called ground control. "Flying Cloud ground this is three niner eight requesting taxi instructions to Aircraft Unlimited."

"You are cleared to taxi direct to requested hanger. Welcome home, Mister Vice-President."

Scotty took the microphone, "All right, you guys. I'm still me so let up or I'll look for hanger space elsewhere."

"Roger that."

Scotty taxied to the front of the hanger and shut everything down. "I'll refuel and push the Lear into the hanger if you'll open up the office. We can unload the office equipment Monday morning, but I want to call Len now."

Scotty topped-of the fuel tanks and backed the Lear into the hanger. After putting away the tow bar and the tug he walked into the office. Grace had a pot of coffee ready and passed a cup to him. He picked up the phone and dialed Len's number.

When Len answered, Scotty asked, "I just heard the news, how come you're selling?"

"Scotty, I hoped you would call. I read the story in today's paper about your promotion. Congratulations. I saw the pictures of the Sopwith and S.E. 5a. You did a great job restoring those two antiques."

"Thanks on both counts, Len. But, don't evade my question. Why are you selling?"

"For two very good reasons, my young friend. One, I'm tired. I want to have some fun, instead of working seven days a week. Two, Barbara is having some health problems, and we want to have some time together. Barb and I are going to take a year and travel. We want to be able to do it at our pace and enjoy the sights and meet the people."

"Is this a serious health problem, Len?"

"It will be if we don't do something about it soon. That's another reason for me to be home. The new owner will take over at the end of the month. The only part of the service we'll be taking with us is the old Cherokee six. Buster is doing a major on the engine and a complete annual now. We bought a small home near where your folks live. However, we won't be there much. Within a few weeks after we turn the service over, we'll be leaving for Europe. After that, who knows?"

"Speaking of Buster, I hear the new owner won't be doing service work. What's Buster going to do?"

"Scotty, I have to tell you, I don't know. He said he might look into getting a job with an airline, but I don't think he'll even try. He might retire."

"Do you think he might consider working for me? I've got an idea in my head and he'd be the perfect choice to head up a new department."

"That would be great, Scotty. I don't think he would turn you down. He's pretty proud of the job you've done. Whatever you have in mind, if it has anything to do with airplanes, I believe he would be right there to help."

What I have in mind is a restoration shop. What do you think?" Scotty said enthusiastically.

"Call him right now. I think he'll jump at the chance."

"I'll do that, Len. While I'm on the subject, how about you? In your travels, keep an eye out for good re-buildable old planes. I'll pay a finders fee, if we buy the planes."

"We'd love to do that for you, Scotty. And, I'm sure Buster will say yes."

"That's great, Len. Give Barb a big hug and kiss from all three of us. Call me, before you leave town."

Scotty dialed Buster's number and waited for the gruff voice to answer, "Yah, what d'ya want?"

"Buster, it's, Scotty."

"Well, it's about time you called me, hot shot. I heard the good news. I'm happy for ya."

"Thanks, Buster. I owe you for most of my knowledge, so you can take a bow for the two bi-planes. And, that's the reason for this call. I just got back from Chicago and the boss has given me permission to begin planning a new venture here in town.

"I want to start a restoration and renovation service department here. As long as Len has sold out, I thought you might be interested. That is, if you don't have something else lined up. I'd like you to come to work for me and head that department. There seems to be a market for some of these old birds and several owners have expressed an interest in having their planes overhauled and up-dated. Do you think you might be interested?"

"Let me think about this awhile. Did Len ask you to call?"

"No, he didn't. I did call him to ask if it would be all right with him if I offered the position to you. I didn't know if you two had something planned."

"Well, if you could take the time to stop and see old friends once in a while, you might find out what's going on."

Scotty smiled, "As usual, you're right, Buster, and I have no excuse. Being busy isn't acceptable. Please think about it, Buster. I really need you to help get this part of the business up and running. Besides, I want you to come out to see our new home and private airport. Grace said she misses your smiling face, and you haven't met Billy yet. I'll be here all next week either at home or here at the airfield. Please call, and thanks for giving my proposal some thought."

"All right, Scotty. Give me a couple days to think it over. I'll come to your office Wednesday afternoon. We'll talk about the whole idea. Then I'll see if I'd be interested. Maybe we can work a deal. Besides, I'm looking forward to seeing Grace, and I want to meet the next generation of MacTavishes."

"Thanks, Buster. We'll be looking forward to your visit."

Scotty looked over at Grace. He nodded and speculated, "He'll be here on Wednesday afternoon. I believe he'll do it. He won't be able to turn it down. I remember how he looked when we took the Bonanza out of the hanger that first time. The paint glistened in the sun, and she looked great. Buster's eyes just shined and his smile was at least a mile wide. Yes, I believe he'll take the job."

Monday morning, Scotty and Grace unpacked the office equipment Ben had packed into the Lear. By mid-morning everything was hooked up and working. Shortly after lunch the telephone company came to bring in a dedicated computer phone line so Grace could work off the company mainframe computer. By mid-afternoon the connection was complete and checked out. Grace signed on and requested several reports to be down loaded to their computer.

Just as the down loading was completed, a radio call came in on the company frequency. "Scotty, this is Ralph. I've got a rough engine, and I'm afraid it'll quit on me. Can I get you to take a look at it?"

"How far away are you, Ralph?"

"I'm about fifty miles northwest of you."

"Okay, call Flying Cloud tower for clearance and shut down the sick engine as soon as you're safely on the ground. I'll have the hanger door open. There's room in the front of the hanger for your plane. Taxi straight in but shut down your good engine just before you enter the hanger. We'll get you going as soon as we can."

"Roger, Scotty, and thanks."

"Scotty, I think I'll leave for home now," Grace said. "I have to take Billy home and get him fed, bathed and ready for bed."

"Good idea, honey. I'll wait for Ralph and get him on his way. I'll call you before I leave here. If you're not home, I'll leave a message on the answering machine."

Twenty minutes later an all-white Cessna twin taxied up to the hanger on one engine.

Scotty rolled his tool chest up to the left engine, put on a pair of thick gloves to protect his hands from the hot metal and began removing the engine cowling.

"By the time I got it on the ground, the engine temperature was almost in the red. As soon as the wheels touched the ground I shut the engine down."

"Good job Ralph. I think all we'll need is a set of plugs. By the way, do you know what the weather forecast is for tomorrow?"

"Yes. It's calling for high pressure with light and variable winds.

"That sounds great. Maybe I'll hitch a ride back to Chicago. I'd like to get the Sopwith home."

Twenty minutes later they had the twin out of the hanger and running the left engine. "Take it up and fly a few miles away, maybe five or ten minutes from the airport. Then come back here. If all's well, you can re-fuel if you need it, then we'll be on our way." Ralph nodded, and Scotty got out of the plane and walked toward the hanger.

He found the overnight bag he always kept ready to go. He packed his open cockpit helmet into its bag along with the face shield earphones and microphone that connects him to the outside world. He picked up the phone and called Grace. She had just arrived home. "Honey, I think I'll fly back with Ralph. I'd like to have the Sopwith in the hanger when Buster comes on Wednesday. The weather is supposed to be just like today. I hope you don't mind."

"I thought you'd come to that conclusion. That's why I left when I did. Have a good flight and be careful. Call me before you leave Chicago."

"Thanks, for understanding, Grace. Give Billy a kiss for me and take one for yourself. I may try to get an early start. I'd like to have lunch with my wife tomorrow."

"I accept your offer to buy lunch, as long as it's not fast food. See you tomorrow."

Scotty walked out of the hanger just as Ralph taxied up to the fuel pump. He stowed his two bags in the luggage compartment while Ralph re-fueled the Cessna.

After landing in Chicago, Ralph took a sleepy Scotty to a motel close to the airport and checked him in. Scotty was back at the hanger at 5:00 the next morning. He received a complete weather briefing and filed his flight plan. A candy bar and a donut from the machine made up his breakfast. He washed both down with a cup of machine coffee.

He went into the hanger and found some help pushing the Sopwith onto the ramp. He took his time walking around the plane and made sure he checked everything. He hadn't looked at it since landing in Chicago. He checked the oil and found it still nice and clean. It wasn't low, so the engine wasn't burning much and he couldn't see any leaks. That was unique for an older plane. The Sopwith didn't come with a fuel gauge. A float under the gas cap with a piece of flying wire protruding through the top of the cap was all he had. He didn't trust that kind of gauge, so he climbed up and took the cap off and looked down into the tank. Sure enough, the crew had re-fueled it.

One of the safety devices he had installed was a petcock in the bottom of the fuel tank. He squatted down and opened the petcock and drained a small amount of gas into a class jar. He was satisfied. He put his helmet on the seat and went into the hanger.

He checked his office for any messages. Some letters were on his desk along with some reports he'd asked for. He tucked them all into the leg pocket of his flight suit. He picked up the phone and called Grace. "I'll be leaving in a few minutes. The weather sounds great. I should be there by one o'clock I think. Pick a nice place for lunch and make a reservation. I'll see you soon."

Scotty took his time when he climbed into the Sopwith and started the engine. Fifteen minutes later he pushed the throttle all the way to the dash and popped into the air. With fifty feet of air under him, he banked off the runway and took the short way off the airport grounds.

He climbed to cruising altitude, activated his flight plan and settled back for a nice comfortable flight to his first fuel stop.

At noon Scotty switched to the company frequency and called Grace. "Go ahead, Scotty. You're coming in loud and clear."

"I should be on the ground in twenty minutes or so. This old bird is just great. It gives you a good look at the countryside with plenty of time to see it. I even had a couple of boys waving to me as I flew by a small town. I'll tell you all about it over lunch. See you soon."

Grace had the hanger door open for him when he taxied up. He cut the engine and coasted into the hanger, and she closed the door. When he climbed down, there was a broad smile on his face. He took her in his arms and gave her a big kiss and said, "The World War I ace returns from battle once again."

Grace laughed and slugged him on the arm. "Welcome home, my brave aviator."

CHAPTER TWENTY

SCOTTY DIDN'T SLEEP THIS TIME. He was determined to stay awake so he could get the first flare in the air. He was sure that someone would see it and investigate. He had twenty-four flares in the cardboard box. If he sent one up every thirty minutes, he should have enough to last for two nights, if he quit at midnight.

He let his mind wander back to the beginning. *Flying has always been in my blood from the first time I saw an airplane. I'm not sure why because we don't have any family in any part of aviation. I remember spending most of my time at the airport watching the planes takeoff and land. It always fascinated me how an airplane can overcome gravity and fly through the air. Even now, after all the education I've had, it still fascinates me.*

It seems like just a few weeks ago I began training with Len. Boy is he going to give me a lecture when he hears about this. I can hear him telling me to do a complete aircraft walk around check. No shortcuts. Check the engine oil and for anything in the engine compartment that doesn't belong there. Get a complete weather briefing and, above all else, make sure you have enough fuel to get to your destination, plus an hour. There is no excuse to justify running out of gas.

Those early years gave me so much happiness. Like the first time I took the controls of that Cessna trainer, my first solo cross-country or my test ride for my license.

Scotty loaded the flare pistol and fired it into the air. The flair burst at the top and a little parachute let the flare down slowly. It lit the open field well enough to see the trees on the far side. He timed the drop at nine minutes.

"That's not bad for this kind of flare. That means nine minutes for someone to notice it." He loaded another flare into the pistol and set it down beside his leg. The pain was beginning to come back in his stomach and arm. His legs were still numb. He slipped his hand under the sleeping bag to see if his toes were warm. They were. "That's one thing I don't need to worry about."

I remember when Buster and Len suggested the emergency kit. I'm glad I put one in the plane and added the flare pistol. Too bad they didn't tell me to put it in the cabin where I could reach it. I should have thought of that myself.

It was time. He brought the flare pistol up and pointed it skyward and fired. The flare burst and lit the clearing. He saw four deer running for cover in the trees.

He watched the flare until it was almost on the ground. There wasn't any wind so the flare landed within a few yards of the first one. His eyes were locked on the far side tree line. He spoke out in a strong voice, "What a dimwit I am. I've been worried if the emergency locator beacon has been working. Why don't I tune to the emergency frequency and see."

He rotated the frequency knob to the locator's frequency and sure enough there it was sending out its beeping message continuously. "That's a relief."

In a very tired voice he asked the next question, "Why haven't I been using the emergency voice channel. He switched to the voice frequency and listened. He didn't hear anything. Just at that moment a spasm of extreme stomach pain hit him and he doubled over and spit up more blood and part of the candy bar he'd eaten. The violence of the episode left him weak, with a raging headache, dizziness, and disorientation.

He groped for and found the microphone. In a very weak voice, "Mayday, this is Bonanza one victor. I'm down on . . . north side . . . small . . . clearing. Hurt badly. Need help, soon. Please respond."

Another spasm, more blood, and much more pain shocked his body. He let his back find the broken stump, then leaned against the side of the plane and finally passed out. A shudder ran through his body that brought him back for a moment. He opened his eyes, looked out at the clearing and closed his eyes again. And he dreamed.

He was looking down on little Billy's crib. He bent over the crib and very tenderly picked Billy up. He cradled him in his arms and kissed both cheeks and then hugged him close. And Billy disappeared. He looked at his empty arms and SCREAMED No!

CHAPTER TWENTY-ONE

S HORTLY AFTER LUNCH ON WEDNESDAY, Buster's beat up old pickup pulled into the parking lot of Aircraft Unlimited. He got out, looked around, and then slowly made his way to the office door. As the door opened, Grace's eyes turned from the computer screen. "Buster, welcome to your new home." She came out from behind her desk and gave him a warm hug. "It's good to see you again. Come on, I'll show you around. Scotty's talking with Ben right now. They're talking business so it could take awhile."

She took him through the office and lunchroom, then into the hanger. She flipped a switch that brought the hanger from twilight to full brightness. Buster's eyes took in everything, from the spotless floor and windows to the neat, clean benches. He saw the drip pans under all four of the well-positioned aircraft. Up near the hanger door against one wall was a rack holding six different tow bars. Buster let a smile creep across his face. "Well, it looks like the kid did learn something after all," he commented.

"The kid, as you call him, is always quoting you. When someone tries to tell him how good he is, Scotty always tells them that what he is and what he knows came from very talented people. He thinks you, Barbara, and Len are the best teachers and his favorite people."

Buster turned and walked toward the Sopwith. As he walked, with Grace trailing behind, he reached up and wiped a little moisture away from his eyes. "Did Scotty do all of the restoration on this bird?"

"No, the plane was already restored. Scotty just disassembled and then reassembled when it came in from Australia. He did change a few things to make it a little more comfortable and safer to fly, like the radio, with a helmet that has the earphones and microphone built into it and an exhaust heat exchanger that allows heat to flow through the cockpit in cold weather."

The door leading to the office opened and Scotty came striding across the hanger floor. "Thanks for coming, Buster. How do you like my little fighter plane? Sorry, no machine guns. I've been thinking about finding one somewhere, or possibly having a non-working replica made."

"I see you haven't scratched up the Bonanza yet. She still looks great. Who belongs to the Lear and the Cessna twin?"

"They're both company planes. The twin is for sale and the Lear is my personal transportation. We have another hanger down the road a short distance that has six other planes waiting for new owners. I've been talking to the airport authority about getting more space or a larger hanger. Come on let's go back to the lunchroom and talk. I'll fill you in on what I would like to do."

When all three were sitting at a table with fresh coffee, Scotty began telling Buster what he had in mind. "After Ben dropped his bombshell last week, he gave me a chance to tell him about my idea for a restoration and renovation shop for all types of aircraft. The company came out well on the S.E. 5a even with the shipping from Australia. From the profits of that one plane he paid for my Sopwith.

"From his experience with his Liberator, what he saw in what you and I did on my Bonanza and the profits he made on the sale of the S.E. 5a, he liked the idea but wanted to know how much business we could generate in a year. I didn't have an answer for him but what I did tell him was that we could do other service work until we got that department up and running.

"We would be doing the small operator and the private pilots a great service now that Len has closed his service shop. Besides, everyone in this area knows your work so we wouldn't have to do a lot of advertising.

"I'd like you to run the shop here. It'd be up to you to set it up the way you want it. The restoration and renovation part of the service we'll advertise on a national level. Ben will be looking for projects during his upcoming European trip. Len told me he would keep an eye out during his post-retirement vacation.

"All airframes will be done here. All major engine work will be done in Chicago, at least in the beginning. They have a beautiful clean room there. Any minor engine work for regular or renovation will still be done here. Any questions so far?"

"One big one, Scotty. Who has final say on what's done during a restoration of a company-owned antique?"

"Primarily you would. However, Ben or I will need to be sold on your assessment and cost figures. So, I guess, it would be a company decision based on your thoughts and ideas. Does that answer your question?"

"If I understand you right, it'd be my sole responsibility to do the parts and labor quote to make the plane airworthy once again. Does that sound about right?"

"That's right. However, we would expect you to tell us if you think it's worth the effort or if we'll be able to get our money back, along with a little profit for our trouble."

"One other thing, do I have the ability to hire help if it's needed?"

"You'll have the authority to run the shop and ask me for help, when you need it. When your request is approved, then you will have the hiring authority. And, Buster, that's not going to be a problem. We're trying to grow the business not hamper it. If you feel you need help, ask for it. If you have someone special you want, tell me about it. We'll do our best to get it done."

"Two more questions and then I'll get out of your hair. How much are you paying? And, when do you want me to start?"

Scotty smiled and answered, "Fifteen percent more than Len paid you and 8:00 Monday morning."

Buster stood up, looked at Grace and bent down and kissed her on the cheek, "See you soon, kid." Then he looked at Scotty with a slight frown on his face. He held out his hand and commented, "You got a deal for at least three years, hot shot. After that, I may retire."

Scotty stood and grasped Buster's outstretched hand and pulled him in for a big hug. "Not, hot shot, you old fart, just Scotty to you." Buster nodded then turned and walked out the door without a word.

Monday morning at 8:00 sharp, Buster's old pickup truck drove up to the big hanger door. He walked into the hanger and opened the door.

Very carefully, he lowered his three-layer, custom painted, and roller-equipped toolbox. He moved it over against the wall near the room that Scotty told him would be his office. He walked back to the truck and retrieved a cardboard box from the front seat, walked back to the office and closed the door.

Ten minutes later, Scotty walked into Buster's office carrying a large plastic bag and saw the wall behind the desk plastered with all of Buster's framed licenses, commendations, and thank you letters. He dropped the plastic bag onto the desk. "Here are your working uniforms. There's six sets so you'll always look like a service manager."

Buster opened the bag and took out one of the white shirts. Looked at the front and saw the Aircraft Unlimited logo and SERVICE MANAGER embroidered under the logo. Below that embroidered in script was his name. "Pretty fancy, ain't it?" he commented.

"That's the same uniform used by the Chicago service people. You're an employee of this company. You're the Minneapolis service manager. It says so right there on your shirt. Change into the uniform when you have a moment."

Buster looked into the bag and pulled out a pair of dark blue pants. While he emptied his pockets and pulled the belt out of his pants he asked, "What do you need me to do first, Scotty?"

"One of the first things I'd like you to do is find us a good one-ton pickup truck. Most likely it should be a diesel. Make sure it's equipped with a good radio, cruise control, air conditioning and whatever else you think it would need for long hauls. Then I want you to find a flat-bed trailer capable of hauling a complete but disassembled aircraft. Maybe twenty-five to thirty feet long. When you find the truck and trailer, give me a call and let me know what it'll cost. Then, I'll make the funds available.

"Right after we get the truck, trailer, licenses, and insurance, be ready to make a trip down to Kansas. Ben found us a Waco PT14 basket case. He wants us to begin a complete restoration to flyable condition. I'm told it's been sitting in a barn for the past thirty years and most of the fabric has rotted off but it's supposed to be complete.

"I expect it'll be a lot worse than the owner said, but Ben said he didn't care what it cost, just get it flying again. So, that's what we'll do. Ben learned to fly in a Waco, and he's a very sentimental person. Look at what he spent on that Liberator. We're going to give him a great little primary trainer to play with.

"Here's the key to my car. It's right outside the front door. Use it to do your running around. Any questions so far?"

"No, not yet. I'll get right on it as soon as I change clothes."

Shortly after lunch, Buster called. "Scotty, I think I found what you're looking for. I'm at a Ford dealership just a few miles away and he has a one-ton, duel wheel, pickup loaded with everything you can imagine. It's been in demonstrator service for the past ten months. The new models are coming out, so it's up for sale. There's only a little over four hundred miles on it, and it looks like new. I drove it and it handles like a dream."

"Sounds like what we need, Buster. What color is it?"

"It's white with a blue interior and the price is right."

"Tell them to make out the paperwork for company ownership. I'll make the arrangements for insurance. Tell them we'll come back tomorrow morning and sign the papers. Have you found a trailer yet?"

"No, that's next. I've got an idea about what we should have for this job but I want to talk to a friend of mine about it. I should have something by late this afternoon."

"Great, Buster. I'll be looking forward to your ideas."

Buster came hustling in just after four o'clock that afternoon. "Scotty, I think we've got the whole outfit that'll do the job we want it to do." He laid a picture on Scotty's desk. It was a picture of a forty-five-foot-long, totally enclosed, fifth wheel trailer.

Buster enthusiastically told Scotty, "It's been hauling my friends' race car for the past few years. It has a complete workshop up in the front part and a double bunk over the fifth wheel.

"I thought an enclosed trailer like this one would be a better deal for us than just a plain flat bed because it would protect whatever we'd be hauling from the wind and weather. Like that basket case Waco we'll need to pick up. We could cause a whole lot more damage to an old plane just from the wind created from traveling as slow as forty miles an hour. With this trailer we could move at the speed limit with no damage at all.

"The back wall of the trailer is one solid piece. It swings down on heavy hinges to form a ramp for loading. It's strong enough to allow something as heavy as a racecar to drive right into the trailer. And, it's high enough for most light planes to be moved in with just the wings removed."

When Buster stopped for a breath, Scotty raised both hands over his head, "I give up. You've sold me. I think it's a great idea. Is this one for sale?"

Buster looked at Scotty with an embarrassed grin on his face. "I guess, maybe, I did get a little over excited. I thought it would be a great idea. Yes it's for sale, but we need to let him know if we want it. He's talkin' about puttin' an add in the racing magazine tomorrow if we don't take it."

"No need to be sorry, Buster. I like to see excitement in people. It's a great idea. I never considered damage could be done on a flat bed. I wouldn't have thought of a covered trailer until the damage had already been done. Is his selling price realistic?"

"Yeah, he told me he'd sell it to us well under the market, because we're friends. He's already depreciated it out for tax purposes. I think it's a great deal and the base color of the trailer is white. We can paint the company logo on the sides and get a little advertising out of it at the same time."

"That's what I like about you, Buster. You're always thinking about the company," Scotty commented. "We can take the cost of repainting the trailer off our taxes as advertising. Great idea. Call your friend and tell him we'll take it. Tomorrow, we'll go to the dealership and pick up the truck. Then, you can take the truck to pick up the trailer. Plan on doing the trailer in the hanger or if you have a friend in the business, take it there to have the painting done. Just let me know."

The next day, Scotty made out checks to pay for the truck and the trailer. And, yes, Buster did have a friend in the business. A week later, the truck and trailer were delivered to Aircraft Unlimited.

Buster had given the painters a picture of Ben's Liberator as a model for the logo that would be painted on the side of the trailer and on the truck doors. Scotty was so impressed that he took pictures with his Polaroid and mailed copies to Chicago.

Buster pulled the truck and trailer into the hanger where it would be out of the sun. He needed to equip the trailer with enough tools to do the disassembly of the Waco. The trailer had a toolbox built into one wall in the forward workshop. A small drill press had been left in the workshop and Buster added a portable welding/cutting torch. Within a few days, Buster announced the truck ready to go.

Scotty asked Buster, "Do you need any help to do this job?"

"I'd like to take my grandson, Stan, along if it's okay with you. We call him Stooge. School doesn't start for another month and I've been working with him for a while. He thinks he would like to be an aircraft mechanic."

"Where does he live, Buster?"

"Just a few miles from me. I can bring him with me when I'm ready to leave."

"How about we put him on the payroll? If you do for him what you did for me, I'd love to have him working for Aircraft Unlimited. How old is he?"

"Seventeen. He'll graduate from high school next year. I've been working with him for the past three years, but he isn't as fast as you. He'll be a good mechanic, but not in your class."

"Buster, I don't believe that. He's old enough to work for us, so I'd like to hire him. We'll start him just like I did, working with you in the shop. He can help with the Waco. Maybe that'll give him a little spark. How far away is he from getting his airframe license?"

He's still at least a year away, but if he works at it a little harder he could be ready by the time he graduates from high school."

"Buster, talk to your son and daughter-in-law and to Stan. If he's serious about being a mechanic, and his parents agree, we'll put him on as an apprentice with the same wages he would get working for an airline. That way, as an employee, he'd be covered by our insurance. I'll add this also—the company has a tuition reimbursement program if he wants to go for a college degree. In any case, I think you'll need the help, so take him along."

"Thanks, Scotty, I think he'd like the chance. I'll talk to Stooge, and, by the way, it's my daughter and son-in-law. If they agree to let him work here, I'll bring him in tomorrow morning and you can explain what will be expected of him. He already has his own tools. We'll bring his tool box with us."

"I'll look forward to meeting him, Buster, and thank your daughter and son-in-law. When, you're talking to them, tell them you'll be leaving Monday morning. I'm thinking it'll take you one long day to get there, three days to dismantle the Waco and get it loaded, and another two days to drive back. That's at least six days if everything goes well. I'll have to get uniforms for Stooge. Do you know if he'd prefer shirt and pants or coveralls and what size he requires?"

"He likes shirts and pants. I'll get his size for you if he takes us up on this chance," Buster answered.

"One other thing, Buster. I'd like you to get another set of tools to stay with the trailer. Make sure you buy enough to do a disassembly of any type aircraft. That way the trailer will be ready to roll at any time."

"I'll get hold of my tool guy. He'll be in seventh heaven. He's a great guy. He'll work with us on anything we need. I'll put together a list of what we'll need and I'll fax it over to him today. He should have everything ready for us by tomorrow afternoon."

"Great, Buster. It looks like we're on our way with this new adventure, and I'm sure it will be an adventure."

The following morning Buster walked into Scotty's office with his coffee cup and sat down. "I talked to my wife and filled her in on our conversation about the Stooge. She was thrilled. She thought it was a great chance for the Stooge. She called our kids and asked them to bring the grandkids and come over for a backyard cookout.

"After we had our dinner of the three B's—burgers, brats and beans—we talked to the whole clan. The Stooge's jaw was on his chest within minutes. Scotty, you have to know by now that the whole family knows about my working with you and the success you've had. They were overjoyed at this chance for the Stooge. It took him all of two seconds to agree. He didn't even look at his parents. But they agreed to let him start next Monday morning.

"I told them, the Stooge and I would be gone at least a week, what we were going to be doing, and that they didn't have to worry about him or buy any special clothes for him because the company would furnish uniforms. So, now we have an apprentice mechanic on staff. Stooge said he'd drive out sometime today for a tour and to sign whatever papers you need signed."

"Did you get his size?"

"He's a big kid. Shirt size is extra large and his pants are thirty-eight waists and thirty-six length. He weighs two hundred twenty-five pounds and plays running back for his high school football team."

Scotty could hear the pride in grandpa Buster's voice but he never cracked a smile. "He's a big guy all right. I'll call Chicago and get his uniforms on the way and get the name, address, and phone number of the Waco's owner. They'll call him and let him know when you'll be getting there.

"Today, I need you to go down to the storage hanger and bring the Cessna 310 up here and that old Piper Apache. The 310 is sold, and we need to make sure it's in good shape and clean. The new owner is coming to pick it up tomorrow. The Apache needs to be checked out and test flown. Grace has a possible buyer coming in on Saturday morning. I'd like to get that one sold. We've had it ever since we opened this office."

Buster stood up, drained his coffee cup and responded, "Consider it done."

The following Monday morning Grandpa Buster and Grandson Stooge, in his brand new Aircraft Unlimited uniform, showed up ready to start their trip to Kansas. Buster and Stooge came into Scotty's office, and Buster asked, "Is there anything special we need to know about this Waco?"

"No. Not that I'm aware of. You have the name, address, and phone number if you run into trouble. When you're finished, why don't you give me a call? I'll make sure you have hanger space to spread out the parts. When you finish unloading, I want you both to take at least two days off. Then I want to hear all about your trip and how it went.

"We'll need to critique the usability of the truck and trailer. We might be using it a lot in the next few years." Scotty shook hands with Buster and Stooge. "Have a safe trip. And, Stooge, you listen to Buster. Some day you might be doing one of these by yourself."

Buster and Stooge filed out of the office in lock step and walked across the hanger and out the big door to the truck. Scotty walked into Grace's office and commented, "Stooge is going to make a great addition to our Aircraft Unlimited family. I think he'll learn very fast, now that he's actually getting paid to learn and to do the job. He's a lot like Buster, in that he's quiet, works hard and gets the job done."

Friday morning, Buster called to say they would be leaving for home within the hour. "Everything went well. The fabric looks like the mice got into it. The seats are trash but the framework is in good condition and the tires are holding air. At least they are for the moment. I don't think it's going to be as big a job as I thought."

"How long do you think it'll take you to drive back?" Scotty asked.

"We should be back at the hanger by Saturday morning. The Stooge wants to drive straight through. Apparently he has a heavy date Saturday night."

Scotty could hear the Stooge object in the background and grinned. "Whatever you do, don't push too hard. Drive carefully. I don't want either of you getting hurt or picking up a speeding ticket. Nothing's worth getting hurt or killed. You know me, Buster, safety first."

"I know, Scotty, and believe me I feel the same way, but there are two of us driving so I believe we can spell each other, and Stooge is a good driver. I should know, I taught him. If we get back before you get in, I'll pull the trailer inside the hanger. We can unload it Monday morning."

"Okay, Buster, but I don't want to see either of you until Tuesday morning. Two days off, remember. And, Buster, just to let you know,

Grace delivered the Apache to her customer yesterday. I took him up for an orientation flight, and he loved the airplane. Good job getting it running so well. Both engines performed perfectly and were easy to synchronize."

"That's great, Scotty. We'll see you Tuesday morning. I'll show you why I feel that the restoration won't be as bad as I thought. Say, hi, to Grace."

Scotty got to the hanger by 7:30 Saturday and the trailer had been backed into the center of the hanger. He opened the back of the trailer and took a quick look inside. The Waco's fuselage had been pushed backwards into the trailer and tied down so it couldn't move. The wings had been padded and strapped to the sidewalls. Everything looked as though it hadn't moved since it had been put into place. Scotty smiled and closed the door.

He went into his office and called the airport manager. After a fifteen-minute conversation, he had a commitment from the manager to install an overhead crane in Aircraft Unlimited storage hanger. All it cost the company was a ten-year extension on their lease. The storage hanger just became the service hanger. Scotty felt good about the progress he had made on the service facility.

CHAPTER TWENTY-TWO

MONDAY MORNING, A MAN WHO IDENTIFIED HIMSELF as Ron Willan, a sales representative for a local crane and hoist company called Scotty for an appointment. "What time can you be here?" Scotty asked.

"I can be there in thirty minutes," he responded.

Thirty minutes later Ron Willan walked into Scotty's office. Scotty explained what he thought he needed in a hoist. Ron asked, "Will you ever need more than five tons lifting capacity?"

Scotty thought for a moment, "I don't think we'll ever need anywhere near that much capacity."

"Can I see the facility?" Ron asked.

"Absolutely. I'll take you now. The quicker we get this accomplished, the better."

Scotty drove him to the storage hanger and they spent about thirty minutes talking about how the hoist would be used and what Ron's company could furnish. Walking out the door Ron said, "I can fax a quote to the airport manager this afternoon and I'll copy you. Our smallest overhead crane will lift two and a half tons. It's a one-man operation, by remote control. It should give you all the lifting power you need."

As soon as we get approval from the airport, I'll send our installation team out to measure the building for the steel beams that'll have to be installed. Then I'll be able to tell you how long it'll take."

"Make sure you give me a few day's notice of when you'll want to begin. I'll need to get everything out of the hanger."

By mid-afternoon, Scotty had a copy of Ron's quote, along with a request for a time when their installation engineer could see the hanger. Scotty called the company and told Ron's secretary that they could come out anytime between 8:00 and 5:00 Monday through Friday and that they should check in at the office.

Scotty was excited. Apparently the airport manager had approved the bid quickly. Things were moving in the right direction and that thrilled him.

Early Tuesday morning, when Buster and grandson Stooge came in, they found a note taped to the back of the trailer. "See me before you unload the trailer. We need to talk about where you want to do the work."

Scotty and Grace arrived at 8:00 and found Buster and Stooge sitting in the office waiting room. "Welcome back, guys. Come into the office. I've got an overhead hoist coming soon. I don't know how long it'll take to install it but it's a good one. It'll reach anywhere in the hanger and is capable of lifting two and a half tons. We should be able to lift just about anything we want with that."

Buster looked at Scotty and asked, "Isn't that overkill? We wouldn't need anything more than, maybe, one and a half tons for the kind of work we'll be doing."

"You're right, Buster. But remember the airport commission is footing the bill for the hoist. I'm sure they're looking at the future if we fold.

"Here's the problem. It'll take them at least two to three weeks to get the hoist installed. We need to begin work on the Waco. They'll need the storage hanger empty for the installation because they're dealing with large metal beams. My question is, can you work in this hanger until we get the hoist installed. Then we'll need to get compressed air, heat and better lighting for you."

Buster thought for a moment, "Sure we can. But let me suggest something else. We already have the wings off. Why don't we check out the engine up here and see what it needs. If Chicago is going to overhaul the engine, let's see what it needs and get it on its way.

"We need to pull the tail section off and peel the fabric so we can inspect the spruce under it. We need to do the same with the fuselage. That won't take us more than two or three days. Then we can take the carcass down to the storage hanger when we're ready to work on it. That way we don't have to spend the money right now to get that building ready to work in."

"We'll need to do it somewhere down the line if Ben has his way," Scotty commented.

"You're right, Scotty, but I have a feeling Ben will be finding more planes for us to refurbish on this vacation of his. And I wouldn't be at all surprised to hear from Len with a project or two. I have a feeling that we'll be loaded within the next month. Two months at the very most."

"Okay, Buster. Unload the Waco and get started on it. We'll move it to the other hanger when the hoist people have finished. I'm going to take the Bonanza and the Sopwith down to the farm this week so they'll be out of the way."

As it turned out Buster's feeling was very prophetic. The next day there was a letter from Ben, asking Scotty to call Willard Cathcart in Australia and ask him if the Fokker Tri-plane was still for sale. If so, what was the price? He said he had a Frenchman who would like to have a real flying Fokker Dr1 Tri-plane for his collection. He wrote that he would call Scotty at the end of the week for an answer.

As Scotty read the letter, he laughed softly to himself. He had told Buster about the Tri-plane and how he had thought Ben would have bought it just to have it around as a bragging piece. Ben never forgot.

True to his word, Ben called from England very early Friday morning. Scotty told him that Willard would sell him the Fokker, disassemble it and take it to the same shipper that moved the Sopwith and S.E. 5a for them. He gave Ben the price, and Ben said, "Call him back today and tell him we'll take it. Have him send it directly to you. Have Buster reassemble it and get it licensed. We'll take pictures of the plane on the ground and in the air. Then we'll send them to France. Get it done, Scotty. This is a big deal for our new venture."

Scotty got it done with a quick call to Willard. Six weeks later the overhead hoist installation was completed, and four weeks after that the Fokker Tri-plane was spread out across the hanger floor of the new restoration facility with Buster looking at all of the parts and a service manual written in German.

"Scotty, how do you expect me to put this thing together and get it licensed without a usable instruction manual? I can't read German, and I don't know enough about these old war birds to do the job right."

"You know enough to put it together. The Germans were good engineers. They should have followed the engineering principles of the times. We'll have to use some current technology to ensure our being able to get it licensed. If necessary, we'll have the manual translated at a later time. Let's see what we can do by ourselves. I'll help you as much as I can.

"I'd like to see us get it ready for pictures in three weeks. Then we can take our time getting it ready for the licensing process."

"Okay, Scotty." Buster turned to his grandson, "Let's get started Stooge."

Later that day, Buster found a note from Willard in one of the boxes. He had saved all of the original hardware and had bagged them in paper bags marked with location and usage. All of a sudden, Buster was a lot more confident about getting the Tri-plane back together.

By the end of the day, the fuselage was sitting on its landing gear and the 110 horsepower Oberursel rotary engine was ready to be bolted to the engine mounts. Two weeks after that, the plane was ready to have its picture taken.

Scotty hired a professional photographer to take the pictures. He took two-dozen photos of the plane inside the hanger and parked on the ramp outside. Scotty ordered four complete sets of prints for distribution to Ben in Europe, Ben's French customer, Chicago, and for his office. Grace put all the pictures into an attractive small album for shipment to Ben and his customer.

Scotty had taken pictures after each day's work. That way he had a daily photographic record of the assembly process. He did the same thing for the Waco, starting with pictures of the plane as it came off the trailer. Grace would make up two albums for each plane when it had been completed. These would be bragging books and sales tools for Chicago and Minneapolis. Grace had made similar books for Scotty's Bonanza, the Sopwith Camel and the S.E.5a. It would make a fine picture history and library of the restoration division of Aircraft Unlimited.

After the photo session was finished, Scotty climbed into the cockpit. With Buster spinning the propeller, they got the engine running.

After just a few minutes of running time, Scotty shut it down. As he dismounted, he commented, "Low oil pressure and a lot of rod noise."

"Yeah, I heard the noise, even over the exhaust noise. What d'ya think?" Buster asked.

"I think we need to box the engine for shipment to the engine shop. I think it needs a complete overhaul."

"I agree with that," Buster said.

They pushed the Fokker back into the hanger and Buster told his grandson to drain the fluids from the engine. Then he followed Scotty into his office.

"What kind of shape is the Fokker in, Buster? What do you see as necessary to complete the renovation process?"

"Only the engine as far as I can tell at this time. Willard wrote in his note that all the wood was in good shape and the fabric was completely new. I might add he did a great job. The cockpit needs some work. I'd like to put in a little better seat. That canvas hammock seat leaves a lot to be desired and some of the instruments haven't been tested.

"For safety sake, I'd like to add an airspeed indicator, a turn and bank indicator and a modern altimeter. Some kind of radio would be helpful. In time, I'd say that all that could be completed in no more than two weeks."

"Great, I'll write a note to Ben with all the numbers and your recommendations. As soon as we get his word, we'll finish the Fokker for delivery. I understand he'll be coming here to take delivery. I hope he isn't planning on flying it back to France.

"As soon as you can, get the Fokker's engine crated. I'll call Chicago to see if a cargo plane will be coming by. As soon as that's done, get Stooge back on the Waco.

"By the way, a flying farmer from southern Iowa read about us in one of the magazines and he's coming up tomorrow with a Stinson Station Wagon. He wants a quote on a complete major overhaul. He's very serious about this because he intends to leave the plane with us. His wife is flying her little two-place Culver mini fighter plane to bring him back. He said if we do a good job on the Stinson, they might have us do the Culver."

Buster sat with a stoic look on his face through this whole discourse, then he commented, "Ya know, Scotty, when you approached me with this project, I thought you were dreaming. I didn't think it had even a remote chance of being successful. I was wrong. It looks like you have a winner on your hands and we'll all be a part of it. Lord, but I'm proud of you." With that little speech he got up and walked out of the office. He left Scotty completely speechless with his mouth open and his lower jaw somewhere down around his belt buckle.

Just before noon the next day, Earl Roberts of Indianola, Iowa, greased a perfect three-point landing in his Stinson Station Wagon. His wife, Nora, did the same in her Culver. They taxied, single file to the ramp where Buster and Stooge were waiting to direct them to a parking spot. They chocked the wheels of both planes, and then Buster introduced himself and escorted Earl and Nora into Scotty's office.

Scotty came around his desk with his right hand extended. "Welcome to Aircraft Unlimited. I'm Brian MacTavish, but please call me Scotty. That's really the only name I answer to." Buster moved toward the door and Scotty stopped him, "Buster, stick around for just a few minutes.

"Nora, Earl, please sit-down and rest from your flight." About that time Grace came through the door and Scotty introduced her to the Roberts.

"Can I get anything for either of you? We have fresh coffee, iced or hot tea, or a soft drink. We may have some left-over sweet rolls we brought in this morning."

Earl spoke up, "First things first. I need to visit your bathroom and then I'd like black coffee."

Nora looked relieved and commented, "I'll follow Earl's lead but I'd like one of those sweet rolls with my coffee."

Grace smiled and led them out of the office. Scotty turned to Buster. "As soon as we've had a chance to find out what they want, Grace and I will take them to lunch. Then you and Stooge can roll the Stinson into the hanger and give it a good going over. Then we'll have, at least, a reasonable idea of what needs to be done. Any quote we give them will have to be for a list of specific work we think needs to be done. We can inform them of anything else we find and what the cost would be."

"That sounds like a good plan to me, Scotty. Try to keep them occupied for at least two hours."

With Nora and Earl back in their chairs, Scotty and Buster asked questions and got a good idea of what they wanted. Then Scotty said, "We'll need some time to look the plane over and run tests. Then we'll be able to give you a good idea of what it'll cost."

Earl broke in, "Scotty, we'd really like to see some of your work in progress and some that has been completed. We made reservations at a motel near your Southdale Shopping Mall. We've never been to a big indoor shopping mall, and Nora wants to do a little shopping. Then we'll come back here tomorrow morning and do the deed."

"That's perfect, Earl. I tell you what, Grace and I will buy you both some lunch, and then we'll take you out to our home. I have a hanger and a short landing strip out there and you can see my Bonanza and the Sopwith Camel we did. But before we leave, you can take a look at the Waco biplane and the Fokker Tri-plane that are in the hanger now. Both are in process, and, yes, that's a real German World War I fighter. Then we'll take you to your motel."

The following morning, over coffee and rolls, Scotty, Grace, and Buster met with Nora and Earl. Buster talked with them about what he had looked at and what he thought needed work. Scotty assured them that the quote they would give them would cover what they intended to do. He also told them that, in the event they found something that they felt needed to be addressed, they would explain what was needed, and the cost, and then get their approval before beginning any additional work.

Earl asked, "Will the engine need a major overhaul?"

"Yes, it will. As a matter of fact, the engine is at least a hundred and fifty hours over the recommended hours since last overhaul," Buster, answered.

"Will that slow down the job?" Nora asked. "We had planned on taking the Stinson to visit our son in Texas over the Christmas holidays."

"As far as we can tell, we should be finished by the first of November. That is if we don't run into anything major, like a cracked wing spar or something like that. The engine will be sent to our Chicago facility because they have all of the tools and a great engine clean room," Buster answered.

Both Nora and Earl brightened up after that and Earl commented, "Sounds great to us. Let's take a look at your proposal."

The four of them spent the next thirty minutes going over the paperwork. With all of his questions answered, Earl signed the work order. Earl and Nora shook hands with Scotty and Buster and moved out to the hanger. Earl collected his flight bag from the Stinson, and Nora retrieved the shopping bags from Grace's office.

Buster and Stooge pushed the Culver out of the hanger and Earl began loading everything into a very small storage area. After goodbyes had been said, Nora fired up the Culver's engine and they were on their way back to Iowa.

As Scotty, Buster, and Stooge watched the Culver race down the runway, Scotty said, "Get the Stinson engine pulled and crated as soon as you can. I'll call Chicago and get a freight stop scheduled. The engine shop is going to have a good time trying to find parts for that Fokker. I'd like to see both engines back well before the first of November."

"I'll get started pulling the Stinson engine. I should be able to have it crated by lunchtime tomorrow. I think we can expect that engine to be completed in a week or so, but the Fokker engine may take a while. They may be able to find parts in Germany, and then again, maybe not," Buster commented.

Scotty nodded and walked toward the office, while Buster moved his toolbox close to the front of the Stinson and Stooge returned to the Waco.

Later that day, Scotty came out of the office to tell Buster, "I just got a call from Len. He's in California. Man, are they moving fast. Anyway, he found a Stearman PT17 at a small private airstrip out in the desert. It still has the original military markings. The owner says it's flyable, but Len thinks it shouldn't be flown.

"He says there are holes in the wings and tail surfaces. He thinks it looks like windstorm or possibly hail damage. Do you think it's something we should be looking at? I'll be talking to Ben later this evening, and if I recommend it, I'm sure he'll give us permission to buy it."

"Absolutely we should. I'll bet we could sell it to a museum just by patching the holes," Buster was quick to point out. "In fact, we could probably sell it to one of the antique plane clubs. In either of those scenarios, we could get a commission to restore it. I know I'd love to get that job."

"Okay, Buster. I'll make the recommendation to Ben when I call him tonight."

"If we get the job, we'll need to hire at least one more mechanic, Scotty."

"I understand. Do you have someone in mind?"

"Yeah, I do. He's an old friend of mine from the Army, I'm sorry, Air Force they call it now. He's the one who taught me a lot about fabrics, paints, and dopes. He'd be a great help in those areas. He's good at doing interiors of cabin planes, too.

"I talked to him a few weeks ago and told him about our organization and he asked me to keep him in mind if we ever need more help. I'd like to have him come in and meet you. He's living in North Dakota, and he still flies his own plane. I believe he has a Bellanca 260. If I'm correct, he could be here in a few hours."

"Give him a call, Buster. Have him fly in next Monday morning. By that time I'll have talked to Ben and should have more information to work with. I hope he's flying a 260. That's a great airplane. It rivals my Bonanza in comfort and performance. Maybe he'll take me for a ride."

At 8:00 a.m. the following Monday morning, Walt Warren taxied his Bellanca onto the ramp, shut down the engine and let the plane coast to a stop right where Buster stood.

The two old warriors shook hands and then, warmly, embraced each other. By the end of the day, Scotty had a chance to fly the Bellanca, and Walt had a job with Aircraft Unlimited restoration division.

When Buster told him about the PT17 Stearman, Walt's eyes brightened up and he commented to Scotty that both Buster and he had cut their eyeteeth on the PT17.

Scotty asked, "When would you like to start, Walt?"
Walt looked down at the floor and thought for a moment, then, as though he was talking to himself he said, "Well, I gotta go home to pack up the few belongings I have. I sold the home right after Emma died and the kids took most of the furniture. I don't have a lease, but I should give them at least a month's notice. I have a few weeks left on this month. Maybe they won't mind if I'm out of there at the end of the month. I'll ask.

"I have an old covered trailer I bought from a U-Haul company a few months ago, and I believe I can get everything in that or the pickup." He looked up at Scotty and continued, "I think, if all goes well, the first of the month sounds about right."

"I tell you what, Walt. I'll fly you back home in my Bonanza and we'll store your Bellanca in our hanger. That way you won't have to worry about how you're going to get your plane here. Will that work for you?"

"That works for me. Thanks, Scotty. When do you want to leave?"

Buster spoke up, "Let me have a few hours off tomorrow, Scotty. I'd like to take Walt out to dinner tonight and then tomorrow morning see if we can find him an apartment somewhere close to me or to the airport."

"That sounds like a good plan, Buster. Then I can fly Walt back early Wednesday morning. Why don't you two take off right now? Have a great visit and Buster, you take him to a good restaurant, not a fast food place."

CHAPTER TWENTY-THREE

SCOTTY'S OWN SCREAMS BROUGHT HIM BACK TO REALITY. Tears were running down his cheeks freely. He let them come. He cried like a lost person. That was what he thought he was at that moment. All he could think of was Billy disappearing from his arms.

He picked up the flare gun and, fumbling with his good hand, slipped a fresh cartridge into the chamber and fired. All while chanting through his tears, "I will not let this happen! I will not let this happen!"

His body began to tremble. At first just a little, and then with increasing speed and violence. His whole body ached, his depression was deepening, and his mind was playing cruel tricks on him. He wanted to sleep, but he was afraid to. He was afraid he wouldn't wake up.

The flare had landed and fizzled out in the snow. He picked up another cartridge and loaded the pistol. His trembling made this job a very slow process. When he had the pistol ready, he lifted his arm and fired into the air. He was tired. He let go and drifted into a deep sleep.

The radio crackled and a voice came over the plane's radio, which was still set to Alexandria flight service, "Alex Flight Service, this is Cessna seven two foxtrot."

"Go ahead two foxtrot."

"I heard your downed aircraft's emergency beacon just a few minutes ago. I saw a flare light up the sky and I think this may be your pilot. I'm circling the location right now if you want to get a fix."

"Thank you seven two foxtrot. We got a fix on your position. How far away are you?"

"About thirty miles south southwest of the airport."

"Thanks a lot seven two foxtrot. You've been a great help. We've got a search crew on the way out there. Alex out."

Scotty didn't hear this conversation. The flare touched down in the clearing and fizzled out.

CHAPTER TWENTY-FOUR

BRIGHT AND EARLY ON THE FIRST OF SEPTEMBER Walt Warren reported for work. Buster outfitted him with uniforms and showed him around both hangers. They unloaded his toolboxes, and Walt was ready for work.

The Waco's fuselage, wings, tail section, and all control surfaces had been stripped of fabric. The seats and interior of the plane were out, and the engine had been removed. Buster took Walt over to where Stooge was working on a wing panel. "Stooge, this is Walt Warren. Walt, this is my grandson Stanley, better known as Stooge.

"I'd like you to take over the restoration of this Waco. Stooge has been doing most of the work on it so far. I haven't had a lot of time to guide him through it but he's been doing a good job. I'd like you to help him get his airframe license.

"Teach him all you know. He's told me he likes the work and would like to be a licensed mechanic. I'd like him to be ready to get his mechanic's license as soon as possible. We need to pass on our knowledge to the youngsters, so that knowledge won't be lost."

"I think that's a great idea, Buster. Sure I'll work with you, Stooge. That must be your grandpa's nickname for you. Am I right?" Walt asked.

Stooge shook hands with Walt and answered, "Yes, sir, it is, but I like it. He's taught me a lot and he's given me a lot of books to study just like he did for Scotty, and look at what he's accomplished. I want to be just like all three of you." Stooge stepped back and blushed, a little.

"That's more than he's said to me at one time since he was born," Buster commented.

"That's all right, Stooge," Walt said very gently. "Here's what we're gonna do. You and I will put this Waco together, and she'll be as good or maybe better than when she was built in that factory in Wichita.

Then, when we get her new license, I'll take you and her up for a check ride."

Buster shook his head and warned, "Scotty generally does all the test flying of these rebuilt birds. I don't know if you're familiar with his reputation, but he's better known in this industry as the boy genius. He had his aeronautical engineering degree by the time he was twenty-one years old."

"Yes, I'm familiar with his reputation, and I also know who taught him most of what he knows. Maybe you've forgotten that I still carry a flight instructor rating and that I taught many young men how to fly and fight in this type of plane."

"We'll have to see what Scotty says when the job's done. I can't guarantee he'll agree to your idea. He may want to fly her first then he might let you take Stooge up," Buster warned.

Through September and the first part of October, business at both locations was brisk. Scotty was forced to spend at least two day's a week in Chicago. Grace had a great six weeks in sales. The Flying Cloud location only had two aircraft left in inventory and Chicago had seven. Scotty spent most of his time on the telephone with dealers in other parts of the country trying to locate aircraft that would have a chance of selling.

Scotty was successful in his bid to bring a church-oriented flight service to Aircraft Unlimited for major service and acquisition of aircraft. Most of the flight service operations were in South America and the islands of the South Pacific.

All the planes going to the South Pacific would be shipped by water. The Chicago office of Aircraft Unlimited would build the shipping containers and have them ready for the freight company to pick up.

The planes going to South America would be delivered to their base of operation by a ferry pilot working for Aircraft Unlimited or by contract pilots hired by the church. It was a major piece of business for Aircraft Unlimited.

Scotty still insisted on test flying all aircraft that went through the Flying Cloud facility. Surprisingly, the Fokker Tri-plane was the first aircraft finished. Chicago had completed the engine overhaul in three weeks. They found a German company that kept an inventory of replacement parts for the old planes of that era. This would open the door to more restorations of early German and French flying machines.

Most of the parts were new but made to the original specification or drawings so the integrity of the plane wouldn't be compromised.

On a beautiful late October day, after flying back from Chicago in his Lear, Scotty took the Fokker up for a test hop. The FAA inspector was still on the premises and wanted to watch the test flight.

Scotty fired up the engine and warmed it up to operating temperature. Buster had installed a radio for pilot safety. Scotty got his weather briefing and taxi instructions. He began to taxi to the active runway, checking control operation while moving down the taxiway. At the end of the runway he called the tower for takeoff permission. The tower responded, "Fokker Tri-plane, we have a twin Beech on short final. As soon as he passes, pull out on the runway and hold for clearance."

"Roger, tower."

As the Beech swept past him, Scotty pulled the Fokker onto the runway and stopped. "Fokker, you are cleared for takeoff. Please execute a right turn as soon as possible. I have a hot P51 Mustang just turning final."

"Roger, tower. Execute immediate right turn after takeoff. Fokker rolling."

Scotty pushed the throttle all the way to the panel, and the little Tri-plane sprang forward. In less than fifty yards it jumped into the air and Scotty pushed the stick and rudder peddle to start his right turn. As he came around, he looked over his shoulder and watched the Mustang pilot grease a three point landing with one of the fastest internal combustion engine airplanes in the Air Force inventory.

He flew south a few miles and did his usual test of left and right turns, slow flight, climbing turns, and landing turns. Scotty climbed to an altitude of 5,000 feet and slowed the plane down to approach speed. He wanted to practice a simulated turn to final approach. He wanted a lot of altitude in case the tri-plane decided to whip into a spin. He was almost caught off guard when the little Fokker stalled on that simulated turn to final and immediately snapped into a spin. Scotty pulled it out after one and a half turns that lost five hundred feet.

That shook him a little; in fact it shook him a lot. If that had happened at the altitude he would have been at in a landing, he wouldn't have had time to recover and he would have crashed. He took back the lost altitude and tried it again. This time, he added a little more speed and everything worked as it should. He switched to the company frequency and called Buster. "This thing is a little unforgiving isn't it. I remember something about it killing a lot of pilots with a low-speed stall during landing. Isn't there something else that caused a lot of deaths?"

"Yes, there is. It also tends to stall during high-speed tight turns of over sixty degrees of bank. Please don't try an overhead three-sixty landing. You could spin in."

"Roger that. Everything checks out great. You did a good job reading that manual, even if it was in German. I'll be right back."

As Scotty turned final, the plane began to wobble. He immediately added power and dropped the nose a little, and the Fokker straightened out just fine. Just to prove a point, he did a wheel landing and didn't let the tail drop until just before he began his turn off the runway.

Buster and Walt were waiting on the ramp when he taxied up. When he shut down the engine Buster, commented, "You handled that stall very well for a young pup."

"You know, guys, this bird handles great in the air. But it sure gets skittish the closer you get to the ground. Now I know why the Germans only gave these planes to certain pilots. They had to be good to survive. I guess I'm glad it's going to a museum collection and not to a flying brother."

Late that evening, Scotty called Ben in Ireland. "Ben, we're almost out of flying inventory. I've called all of our past suppliers and can't find much. We need everything. We have two planes here, a single engine and a light twin. Chicago has seven, two singles, three light twins, and two DC3s.

"We also closed the deal with the church flying service, and they want us to find eight planes. Between the two locations we can't supply any of the single-engine requirements, but we can supply the twin-engine planes they want, but then we won't have any light twins left at either location. Any ideas come to mind?"

"Get copies of Chicago, Minneapolis, St. Paul, New York, Boston, St. Louis, and Los Angeles Sunday papers and begin calling on the want ad listings. Also, talk to owners or managers of flight service stations in major markets. That should get you some pretty good leads."

"Thanks, Ben. Oh, by the way, the Fokker is done. I flew it this afternoon and the inspector was there to watch. He passed it, and we now have a certificate. It's ready to be picked up by its new owner.

"We should have the Stinson completed in a week or so, and the Waco will be finished in about three to four weeks. Walt is working out very well, and the job he's doing on the Waco is superb. We now have the Stearman in the hanger and work will begin as soon as the Stinson is delivered."

"Will the Stearman require a lot of rework?" Ben asked.

"The engine will need a top end, and it'll need to be completely recovered. What we can see of the framework seems to be pretty good. We'll know more after we peel the old fabric off. Nora may leave her Culver for restoration when she and Earl come to pick up the Stinson. If she does, we'll have the two planes going. That'll keep the shop busy for a few weeks."

"It sounds like you're doing just fine," Ben commented. "I may need you to fly over to Scotland in a few days. I'm working on picking up a few old birds for your shop. I'll call you sometime next week."

On that note Ben pulled his usual trick and hung up before Scotty could say anything. When he told Grace about the trip to Scotland, she just rolled her eyes and shook her head. "Don't you have enough to do without another international trip? I think you're already spread too thin."

The following Monday morning, Scotty flew to Chicago to complete the paperwork for the four twin-engine planes for the church group. They turned down the single engine planes Scotty had in stock. Their manager told Scotty they wanted a Cessna. Scotty would have to do some searching to find them. However, the Cessna was a popular single engine plane, and it shouldn't be too difficult.

Ben had called and told the office manager in Chicago to book passage for Scotty to Edinburgh Scotland and to cable him with the flight information. The office manager gave Scotty the good news as soon as he walked into the office. He was booked on the midnight flight to New York and would leave on the overseas flight at 6:00 a.m. that morning. This time it was Scotty who rolled his eyes and shook his head as he walked into his office.

"Grace, I need a big favor," Scotty said when she answered the phone. "I need you to pack enough clothes for a week and make sure you pick up my passport. I'll be leaving Chicago at midnight for Scotland. I'll fly back to the house as soon as I finish the paper work on the four twins.

"Why don't you make reservations for dinner? I'll take you and Billy out to dinner and then fly back to Chicago in time to catch my flight. The treats will be on me."

Grace agreed to do as he asked. But as soon as she hung up the phone, she commented under her breath, "Here we go again."

She stood up and walked out to the hanger and told Buster he would be in charge for the rest of the day, then filled him in on Scotty's call to Scotland. Slowly she walked out to her car and drove home. Grace was not a happy camper.

Late that afternoon, Scotty landed the Lear in his cow pasture landing strip and taxied back to the hanger. He felt really tired and put out with Ben for commanding him to fly to Scotland on such short notice.

Grace took one look at him when he walked in the door and immediately regretted her anger. She took Scotty by the hand and walked him into the living room. "You look exhausted. Lie down on the couch for a while. Billy and I will play in his bedroom. I'll come down and wake you in an hour or so. Dinner can wait that long."

"Thanks Grace, I am tired. Chicago is running out of planes, we still need to find two more Cessna single-engine planes for the church group. The shop in Chicago is swamped with work and the pilots want to know when they'll be getting more work. Running both these companies is just too damn much for one man. I'm beginning to understand what Ben went through and why he promoted me. Now, I have this trip overseas, and I'm just not sure why. At least I'll be able to get a good four hours sleep on my way across the Atlantic."

Grace pulled the drapes over the living room windows and turned out the light. "Get some rest. We'll talk more over dinner. I called the steak house over on the highway and they reserved a table for us. We don't have to be there for at least two hours." Grace saw Scotty was already asleep and quietly left the room.

By seven that evening, Grace, Billy, and Scotty were sitting at a table in the steak house. Scotty was filling Grace in on his day in Chicago. She couldn't be angry with him, but she was very angry with Ben. When the meal came, shoptalk stopped and family talk began.

Grace told Scotty about all the things they were both missing as Billy grew. "Scotty, the baby sitter told me Billy pulled himself up and took a few steps today. It won't be long till he'll want to learn how to fly. We really need to spend more time at home because we're missing out on the fun parts of being a parent. When you get to Scotland, tell Ben you need another vacation and soon. Ask him to get you some help, like an assistant marketing manager in Chicago to take some of the aircraft inventory pressure off you. It'll let you have a little more time with both of us. Tell him, if he doesn't, I'll quit."

"Oh, Grace. Honey, you can't do that. Don't even think like that. I don't know what I'd do without you taking care of business when I have to be gone."

"No, I won't do that to you. But threaten him anyway. Maybe he'll get the message."

At ten that evening, Scotty had the Lear loaded with his luggage, and his passport was in his pocket. He kissed Grace and Billy and promised her he'd call as soon as he knew what was going on and when she could expect him.

Grace, with Billy in her arms, watched Scotty walk out to the Lear and climb in. Soon, the engines were running and he began taxiing to the end of the runway. She could follow the plane by watching his clearance lights and landing lights. At the end on the runway, he turned and began his takeoff roll. As he climbed to altitude, she watched his lights in the night sky and wished him well. In her mind, she could see him pick up the microphone and call Flight Service to file a flight plan to Chicago. She pulled Billy closer to her and, softly, kissed his cheek.

Early the next morning, after his flight into New York, Scotty boarded the BOAC flight to Scotland. When the flight arrived at its cruising altitude, the flight attendant came by with coffee and breakfast. Scotty skipped the coffee, wolfed down the breakfast, then reclined his seat and got some much needed sleep.

Ben met Scotty at the Glasgow airport. They went immediately to the hotel where Ben and his wife were staying. Scotty checked in and had his luggage taken up to his room. He and Ben went into the coffee shop and ordered a light meal.

Scotty turned to Ben and asked, "Okay, what's so important that I had to make a rush flight to Scotland?"

"Well, here's the deal. I've been trying to find old aircraft for you and your crew to restore. It appears to be a very lucrative business. I found this P47 Thunderbolt at an abandoned airport on the channel side of England.

"Story is, the pilot managed to get his shot up P47 back to his airfield. Just as he arrived over the airport his engine caught fire and quit. His hydraulic system had been damaged and he couldn't get his landing gear down. So he brought it in on its belly. In any case, a few days later, the invasion of Normandy happened and everyone got busy.

"The plane's been sitting there ever since. The English want it removed, and the Americans didn't know what to do with it. I bought the plane for a dollar, but the catch is I have to get it out of England in a month. That's where you come in, Scotty. You have the knowledge and I've got tools, equipment, and people to help you get it ready to ship.

"I've already got a shipper here in England that'll crate it and ship it back to New York. The papers have all been signed and everything's in order. How long do you think it'll take?"

"It's hard to say, Ben. It'll depend on how much damage there is and how much damage rust and corrosion has done. Let's take a look at it as soon as we can."

THREE HOURS LATER Scotty, Ben, and their pilot were looking over the wreckage of a World War II P47 Thunderbolt. Scotty walked completely around the plane then climbed up on the wing, walking from fuselage to wing tip. He walked back to the cockpit, with the canopy still open, and looked in.

"It can be done, but it won't be easy. Ben, I don't know if it will even be worth it. The shipping costs will be terrific. Yeah, with the proper tools and a little help, I think we can get it disassembled and ready to move in a week, maybe a week and a half."

"That's great, Scotty. I've got three guys to help you. They were all aircraft mechanics during and after the war. I've rented a self-propelled crane to handle the heavy pieces. The people and crane will be here tomorrow morning.

"I've made arrangements for you at a bed and breakfast in the village, and a rental car is waiting back at the hotel."

"It sounds like you have all your ducks lined up. Well, let's get back. I want to be ready to go to work tomorrow morning. Can I drive back here in that time frame?" Scotty asked.

"It should take you no more then four hours to make the drive," their pilot answered."

On the flight back to the airport, Scotty quizzed Ben. "The church group cleaned us out of light twins and most of our single-engine inventory is gone. Grace sold two of our large twins and one small jet. She even tried to sell the company's Lear."

"Scotty, that's not a bad idea. The Lear is piling up a lot of hours. Why don't you let her sell it? As soon as you get back, order a new Lear and equip it the same way. Then have it delivered to Flying Cloud."

At 8:00 the next morning, Scotty showed up at the P47 site to find three men and a self-propelled crane already at work. Scotty introduced himself and pitched in to help. In an hour the engine had been removed and the three helpers had begun building wooden cribbing to elevate the rest of the plane.

At the end of the second day, Scotty called Ben to report on their progress. "I don't know where you got these guys, but they're the best workers I've ever known. They're fast, accurate and very knowledgeable. I wish we had them working for us. I know I could make use of them in the restoration shop. Anyway, call the shipper and have them send out their truck by day after tomorrow. We'll have everything disassembled by that time and we can use the crane to load the truck."

"Great job, Scotty. I called Grace last night and told her to find a home for your Lear. She told me she picked up three light twins from a dealer in St. Louis and Buster quoted three new restoration jobs. She'd like you to call tonight so she can fill you in on the details."

"I'll give her a call as soon as we hang up. Now I know I could use at least one or two of my helpers in the shop."

"I'll call the shipper in the morning, Scotty. He told me he could respond with one day's notice. Besides, he has a lot of political pressure being exerted to get the Thunderbolt out of the country. I'll fly out to the site the day you load up. I'll talk to your crew and see if they would like to come to the United States."

"That sounds good. Even if I can't use all of them, I know Chicago can use them.

Eight days after he had left the farm, Scotty brought the control yoke back, slowly, and flared the Lear into a soft landing on the snow-packed grass strip. He was home. He taxied the Lear up close to the hanger, shut the engines down and climbed out of the plane. He attached the tow bar to the tractor and to the Lear and backed the plane into the hanger. He'd fly it back to the airport tomorrow morning.

Grace met him at the door with Billy in one arm and the phone in her free hand. "It's Chicago. They're running out of planes."

Scotty kissed Grace and Billy and accepted the phone from her. "I know you're running out of things to sell, but I've been out of the country helping Ben with another of his projects.

"Look, it's almost Christmas, I've been working my fingers to the bone for the past two weeks straight, it's late on a Friday afternoon, and I'm tired. I'm going to take this weekend to spend time with my family. We'll work on flying inventory Monday morning. Now, is there anything else on your mind?"

There was a soft chuckle at the other end of the line, then the Chicago general manager commented, "You sound a little tight lipped, Scotty. Are things piling up on you?"

"I'm sorry, Ted. I didn't mean to sound that way. It's just because it's been a long two weeks with a lot of miles under the wings. I just need some time to come down for a soft landing. As long as I've got you on the line, and Grace is standing right here, I'll tell you both that Ben has authorized us to sell the Lear and order a new one.

"Grace and I will fly down sometime next week. At that time, I'd like to have a meeting with you and as many pilots as you can make available. I want some input from all of you on what equipment we should order for the new Lear. I'll let you know, on Monday, when we'll fly in."

"Look, Scotty, I just wanted to let you know that we are running low on flying inventory. I don't like to let that inventory go below six airplanes. Right now we're down to three, two light twins and an old DC4 cargo plane. We could use at least another twelve planes."

"I know, Ted. We're down to just our own Lear, and we could use six or eight here. By the way, Grace has a client that's interested in a small jet for his business. I'm sure she'll be calling him sometime on Monday.

"We'll bring the Lear to Chicago next week. I want you to give it a thorough going over and cleaning before we show it. Maybe I'll bring back one of the light twins, just so we have something here to sell. Unless something else comes up, I'll plan to visit some of the dealers we've done business with in the past, probably sometime in mid January."

"That sounds like a good plan, Scotty. I'll be talking to you next week. Get some rest and give Grace and Billy a big kiss from all of us here in the windy city."

Bright and early Monday morning, Grace and Scotty divided a list of dealers they had worked with in the past. Some of them Grace had contacted a few weeks earlier. Scotty found several possibilities in St. Louis and Kansas City. He made appointments for Thursday with three dealers in St. Louis and four in Kansas City on Friday.

Grace had found some consignment dealers in Wisconsin, Michigan, and Illinois that had some light single-engine planes that had been brought in over the past few weeks. She told the people that she would call back to set up appointments sometime in mid-January. With that information, Scotty began breathing a little easier.

Scotty called Chicago next. "Ted, I think we may have found a few planes in St. Louis and Kansas City. Grace and I will be coming down on Wednesday morning with the Lear. After we have our meeting with the pilots, I want to have a meeting with you and your shop manager. Then, I'd like to take one of the twins. Have it serviced and ready to go that afternoon. I'll be using it to keep my appointments Thursday and Friday.

"Have your pilots ready to go those two days. I'm hoping to find at least two or three each day. Is there anything at your end I should know about?"

"Not a thing, Scotty. Just have a great flight down, and we'll see you Wednesday morning."

Tuesday morning Scotty called Buster in to talk about the workload in the shop. "With no planes in the sales department to worry about," Buster commented, "we're making great time on our restorations. We'll be through with the Culver at least two weeks early. I got a call from the shipper in England yesterday. He told me the Thunderbolt will be loaded on the ship early next week, and the ship is set to sail by the end of the week.

Two J-3 Cubs are sitting in the hanger waiting for us. Both owners said to take our time. They don't need them before next summer. One of those will require an engine major and new fabric. The second one will go quickly because there isn't much wrong with it. The owner has taken care of it. He bought the plane new and picked it up at the Piper factory. That old bird has over ten thousand hours on her and she still looks great.

"While you're in Chicago will you find out the status of the Waco's engine? We'll be ready to mount it in a couple weeks. Walt wants to fly her when we finish. I told him you like to do the first flight on all restorations and major overhauls but you might let him do a second flight. He wants to take Stooge up in it, also."

"You told him right, Buster. I still want to do all first test flights. I know he's a certified instructor in type, and I respect that, but it's my responsibility to take the risks.

"Tell him I'll do the first test flight, he can do a second flight and if all is normal, he can take Stooge on the third flight. That is if you agree. Let's face it, Stooge is your grandson and you should have the last say on that subject.

"Last thing on my mind today is people. Do you think you'll require any more help in our shop? Remember you have a big job coming from England, and I don't know what Ben has in mind for this plane. I don't know if it will be a static display or a flying display. Lacking any information from Ben, we'll be looking at a major restoration to flying status."

"I understand. At this stage, I think we could use at least one and maybe two mechanics to handle routine service of inventory and service from outside the company. I believe Walt, Stooge, and I can handle the restoration side of the business, at least for now. If we get many more jobs, we might need someone, but not at this time."

CHAPTER TWENTY-FIVE

S COTTY WOKE UP RETCHING AGAIN. He brought up less blood this
time and some of it was in the form of clots. "Maybe the internal
bleeding is stopping. I hope it is. At least the stomach pains have slowed
down each time I throw up. But, it sure doesn't help my headache.

"I don't think I slept very long. I need to keep myself awake. I sure
don't want to freeze to death. Not after what I've survived so far." He
picked up the flare pistol and a fresh cartridge, loaded it and fired. This
time the recoil of the pistol hurt his wrist and it dropped to the ground
a few feet away.

He tried to retrieve it but it had fallen just out of his reach. He
leaned toward it and stretched as far as he could. The pain it created
caused him to straighten up quickly. He became disoriented. Everything
seemed spinning out of control. His vision faded and breathing became
shallow and difficult.

He leaned back against the tree stump and closed his eyes until the
pains subsided. He opened his eyes again. The flare was still descending
slowly. He looked around to find something to coax the flare pistol a little closer.

A branch was lying right next to his leg. It had a broken branch
stub at one end. It should make a good hook. He picked up the branch
and reached for the pistol. He hooked the stub into the trigger guard
and carefully pulled it back.

When he had the pistol beside his leg again he relaxed and let the
pains subside. By this time the flare had worked it's way down to the
tree line. He carefully picked up the pistol and extracted the spent shell
and replaced it with a fresh one and set the pistol down in his lap.

*I'm getting so very tired. This constant pain is taking its toll. I'm having
a problem concentrating on helping myself. I know I started to do something*

a few minutes ago but now I can't think what it was. Somebody's trying to tell me something, but I can't hear what's being said. "Oh,—it's the radio in the cockpit. The volume is too low. Concentrate. He's saying s-s-something about me. I can't hear." He slumped and the tears came again.

He picked up the pistol and fired it again. This time he held on tight.

CHAPTER TWENTY-SIX

Grace and Scotty left Chicago early Wednesday afternoon in an older model Piper Apache twin. Scotty was pleased with the performance during take-off. This was a perfect twin-engine plane for some of the shorter grass strips around the country. In fact, this one had belonged to a flying farmer in Southern Illinois and was flown from his twenty-five-hundred-foot grass strip most of its life.

By mid-afternoon the Piper had been put into the hanger at the farm and Scotty was on the phone with Buster. "The Waco engine should be back to us in ten days according to Ted. He told me that it wasn't in bad shape at all. They did have to replace a couple of cylinders but that's all. Ted wants to take a ride in it. It seems like he learned to fly in a Waco while he was in the Army, just before World War II. I gave Ted a heads up on the Thunderbolt engine he would soon be getting. He just smiled.

"Grace will be in tomorrow morning, but I won't be back until sometime late Friday afternoon or early evening. I'll be coming to Flying Cloud because the farm field isn't lighted so leave a spot in the hanger for the Piper. Anything I should know about at your end?"

"Nothing you need to worry about. I started one of the J3s this morning, and the third restoration I bid came in by truck this morning. I had them unload it at the storage hanger because I didn't have room in the service hanger. It's a Piper Tri-Pacer that's been stored in a barn for the past eight years.

"The owner was the young son of a Missouri farmer. He had flown in for a weekend visit and didn't tie the plane down when he landed. That night they had a good old-fashioned rainstorm with high winds. The next morning, they found the Tri-Pacer rolled into a ball up against the barn. The son had no insurance on the plane, so they moved it into one corner of the barn and there it sat until the son could pay off the loan.

"Now he wants us to put it back together. I told him it will be a long and expensive project but he said he didn't care. He just wants to fly it again. I wrote the estimate on a cost plus parts basis and told him it would take at least a year. He never batted an eye."

"Good job, Buster. It looks like we'll need help. We'll talk more next week. I'm hoping things will slow down for me. Christmas is only a little over a week away and I haven't done any shopping yet. Maybe I'll see you Friday afternoon. I'll be calling Grace every day, so let her know if you need to talk to me."

With business over, Scotty walked into the living room and lifted Billy out of his playpen, gave him a hug and kissed his rosy cheeks. "Let's go see what Mom is doing in the kitchen. Maybe she's making some dinner for her two guys."

Scotty walked into the kitchen and Billy let out a squeal of pleasure when he saw Grace. She turned her head to look and commented, "Now, isn't that just a great picture of family togetherness? What are you guys looking for?"

"We're just trying to find out what's for dinner, Mom."

"I haven't figured that out yet. Why don't you guys go back in the living room and play and I'll see what I can find."

At 6:00 the next morning, Scotty was in the barn putting portable heaters on both of the Piper's engines. It was fifteen degrees below zero, and he knew the engines wouldn't start without being warmed up. An hour later, after a good breakfast and a very slow and thorough pre-flight of the Piper, Scotty pulled it out of the barn and had no problem starting both engines. He let them come up to operating temperature before taxiing to the end of the runway.

The weather forecast was good, if cold—clear skies, light and variable winds, and a predicted high temperature of five degrees below zero. Well, it should be warmer in Missouri and Kansas. With that thought, he dropped the flaps a little and advanced the throttles to full power. The Piper rushed down the snow-covered runway and popped into the air.

By 10:00. Scotty had purchased three, single-engine Piper Cherokee 140s and one single-engine Cherokee six-place from three different
dealers/brokers. He was told by one of the dealers that there might be
more available after the first of the year.

He called Ted in Chicago and asked him to send pilots to fly them
to Chicago. Then he added, "As soon as you get them done, send two of
the 140s and the six to Minneapolis. The church group might be interested in them. I'd like to get their requirements satisfied before the end
of the year. That could develop into an on-going search for good light
planes for them.

"I'm going to be leaving for Kansas City in a few minutes. As soon
as I find out what's available there, I'll call."

When he arrived at his next stop, he tied the Piper Apache down
on the ramp of one of the dealers. He took the time to look at his inventory and talked to the owner and made a quick deal for four Cessna
aircraft, all of them single-engines—three were four place and one two
place. The dealer took him to a motel close to the airport.

He called Grace as soon as he could. He caught her at the hanger.
"We have three planes coming as soon as Ted can get them cleaned up
and flown up to us. Have Buster put them in the storage hanger when
they get there.

"Call your church group and tell them we found some planes they
might be interested in. I found four Cessna single-engines if they don't
like what we have. We'll let Chicago have those for now. Maybe I'll be
able to find a few more tomorrow. The way this trip is going, I should
be home mid-afternoon tomorrow."

"You can't get back too soon for me. And, I'm going to put my foot
down. No more traveling until after the first of the year. Now that we
have more people slaving for us, I think it's only to our advantage that
we have some kind of Christmas party for them and their families."

"That's a great idea, Grace. Work something up and we'll talk about
it over dinner tomorrow. Make sure it's someplace we can take Billy.
Anywhere you want to go, just make reservations for three."

"I'll take care of it, boss. Just like the dutiful secretary I am."

"Don't get smart with me, young lady. I can always fire you, ya know."

"Threats and unkept promises, that's all I ever get," Grace commented through a broad smile.

The next morning, Scotty visited two dealers at the same airport and made deals on seven more aircraft, three of which were light twins. *This trip has been successful,* he thought. *It sure will take some pressure off me.* At the last dealer, he placed a call to Ted and gave him the information on all seven planes. Then he bummed a ride back to pick up the Apache.

He did a quick but thorough pre-flight, he made sure that all three fuel tanks were full and checked all three tanks for contaminants. Then he climbed in and started the engines. He filed his flight plan by radio while the engines came up to temperature then called the tower for taxi instructions. By the time he had reached the end of the runway, he had completed his pre-flight checklist.

The tower gave him clearance immediately. He advanced the throttles, turned onto the runway and pushed the throttles wide open. He and the Apache began rolling down the runway and when they reached takeoff speed, Scotty, gently, pulled back on the control yoke and eased the Apache into the air. He was on his way home.

Over the next few days, with Grace's help, Scotty was able to get caught up on his year-end paperwork. The whole crew of the Minneapolis office of Aircraft Unlimited, including little Billy, enjoyed a great Christmas party in the hanger Friday morning. Grace had made arrangements with a catering company for the food then she had purchased gifts for everyone. Just before noon, Scotty told the crew to go home and enjoy the holiday with their families.

Grace had made arrangements with a catering company in Chicago to have food delivered to the hanger in Chicago at 1:30 p.m. for their party. Scotty and Grace loaded the baggage compartment and the back seat of the Apache with gifts for a flight to Chicago. Grace made room for Billy's car seat and made sure it was buckled in very tight. Then she handed Scotty a large box and directed him to put on the costume he would find inside. He came out of his office looking like a very skinny, underfed, Santa.

Grace put Billy into his car seat and buckled him in. This wasn't the first time Billy had flown. By now, he was an old hand at riding in the back seat of an airplane and he was excited to be on the move.

Scotty towed the plane out of the hanger, took the tug and tow bar back into the hanger and closed the door. He climbed into the left seat. Grace settled into the right seat and closed the door. With both engines running, Grace called the tower and received taxi instructions.

Ever since the day she was hired when she made her first trip to Chicago, Scotty had begun training Grace to be a copilot. He wanted her to get her pilot's license. She did have her student's license and she had been taking instruction from a flight training school located on the field. She was ready for the check ride but had decided to put it off until after the first of the year.

They reached the end of the runway and Scotty said, "We're ready."

Grace picked up the microphone and announced, "Flying Cloud tower, this is Apache forty four bravo, requesting take off clearance for Santa Claus and two passengers, direct to Chicago, over."

"Forty four bravo, Santa and family are cleared for immediate take-off. Have a safe flight and thanks for the goodies, Misses Claus."

"You're welcome, guys. Forty four bravo is rolling," Grace responded.

Scotty asked, as he pulled back on the control yoke, "What's with the goodies?"

"I sent enough food over to the tower for the people on duty today, along with a small gift from us. Not the company. I thought they deserved something for all of their hard work on our behalf," Grace answered.

Scotty looked over at her, smiled, touched her arm and, simply, said, "Thanks."

After a few minutes of peace and quiet, Scotty said, "You know, Grace, I'm the boss now. We don't need another manager for Chicago. Ted does a great job. I'm going to give him the authority to be that manager. I'm going to give him the responsibility for flying inventory for the company. He has more time then I do right now. I'll finish it this time but then he'll have to take it over until Ben returns."

Grace smiled and said, "It's about time you came to that conclusion."

Just before two o'clock, when they were on the ground and had their taxi instructions, Grace switched to the company frequency and commanded, "Open the hanger doors. Santa is here."

The big hanger doors began opening. Scotty shut the engines down as he taxied the plane directly into the center of the building and the doors closed behind him.

Grace, with Billy in her arms exited the plane first. Then, Scotty climbed out to applause, whistles, and a lot of shouts. He waved to everyone and then reached into the back seat and began pulling wrapped packages out and handing them to whoever was there.

When all of the gifts had been given out, Ted stepped to a microphone that had been set up near the back of the hanger, "Let's hear it for Santa!"

A loud cheer went up, and Scotty shook hands with Ted and spoke into the microphone as he took off his cap and fake beard, "The last time I was up here I got a new old plane and a lot of responsibility." That brought a laugh from the crew.

He continued, "Did you all get enough to eat?" A loud yes! Came back to him. "And did everyone get a gift?" Again a loud YES! Scotty put his hands up for quiet.

"The next time you see Ben, I would really appreciate it if you would take the time to thank him for this party and the gifts. For a man whose religion doesn't recognize or celebrate the Christian Christmas, he understands its importance to the Christians. This is his gift to us. Our gift to him should be our love, loyalty, and continued hard work.

"And my gratitude for that hard work and loyalty. I thank you all for making my job a lot easier. Now, Aircraft Unlimited is closed for the next four days. Go home to your families and celebrate this holiday season, whatever your religion, and remember Ben and his family in your prayers."

Someone shouted, "Where is Ben?"

Scotty stepped back to the microphone, "I believe he's celebrating the Jewish holy days in Israel with his family."

Grace, Billy, and Scotty, followed Ted to his office for a short meeting and then rolled the Apache out of the hanger for the flight back to the farm and their own Christmas celebration.

During the week between Christmas and New Year, Chicago came for the Apache. They had a customer for it and they didn't bring a replacement. This left Scotty without a company plane. That meant he would have to use his Bonanza if he had to go anywhere because Grace had sold all three Piper 140s and the Cherokee six to the church group.

Once again Minneapolis was without a plane to sell. The entire inventory was in Chicago, including the Lear, and Ted wasn't about to let go of anything, unless there was a deal on it in Minneapolis.

On the third day of the New Year, Scotty spent the better part of the day on the phone, trying to find someone with too much inventory of light planes. The St. Louis dealer, who had told Scotty there might be more planes after the first of the year, came through with four single-engine planes. Three Cessna 150s and a Musketeer. That would help take some pressure off.

He talked to dealers in Minnesota, Iowa, North and South Dakota, Wisconsin, and Illinois. He had been told that there were planes available in all six states. He laid out a big jagged circle starting in Iowa and ending in Illinois. He told the dealers to expect him sometime in the second and third weeks of January.

On the Monday morning of the second week of January, Scotty taxied his beloved Bonanza to the end of the runway to begin his buying trip. That first day he bought six planes, two in Mason City, Iowa, and four in Des Moines. He was finished with all of the dealers he had wanted to see in Iowa by 3:00 p.m. He had intended to stay overnight in Des Moines, but, because it was so early, he flew to Rapid City, South Dakota. That should shorten up this buying trip, at least a little.

Scotty parked his Bonanza on the ramp of the Beechcraft dealer. He walked into the line office and asked for the sales manager. An older man came out of an office to one side of the desk. He was a short, slight, man with a shock of silver-gray hair and dressed in jeans and a sweatshirt with the logo of the dealership printed on the front. He held out his hand and introduced himself, "Hi, I'm Bill Aliston. I own this place. I'm also the sales manager, service manager, one of the mechanics, flight instructor, and chief cook and bottle washer. What can I do for you?"

"I'm Scotty MacTavish with Aircraft Unlimited. I believe I talked with you on the phone last week. You told me you might have some planes you'd be willing to part with."

"Oh, yeah I read about you. You're that boy genius wonder. Yeah. It's good to meet you and, yes, I do have inventory I'd like to move. Come on. We'll go out to the hanger, and I'll show you. Is that your Bonanza out on the ramp?"

"Yes it is. That was my first restoration project."

"It's a 1947 model isn't it?" Bill asked.

"Yes. It's serial number 649, and it's been restored almost to factory original. I did some things to make it a little more comfortable. It has adjustable front seats in both vertical and fore and aft, a tape cassette and a newer style radio.

""I'd like to take a close look at it before you leave. I've got a twin to it sitting at the back of one of my storage hangers. I've had that old Bonanza for six years and haven't been able to find a buyer for it."

"I tell you what, Bill. When we get through looking at your planes, I'd like to see that old Bonanza. We've just opened our restoration facility at Flying Cloud. If the price is right, maybe we can make a deal on it. Why don't you have your line crew wheel my plane into your hanger? That way when we finish our business, you can take your time looking at it where it's warm and we won't have to pre-heat the engine to get it started tomorrow morning."

"Sounds like a great idea to me." He turned to one of his people at the counter and ordered, "Julie, have Randy move that Bonanza into the hanger to warm up. It'll be here overnight, so have him put it toward the front and near a power outlet."

Bill and Scotty walked over to a cold storage hanger and Bill pointed out some of the planes that he would like to move. "I've got three Beech Barons. In this market, I couldn't move that many Barons in three years. You can have at least two of them."

Scotty took notes as they moved through the hanger. They walked to a second hanger and repeated the procedure. When they left that hanger, Scotty had twelve airplanes he was interested in. They moved outside to a series of smaller hangers, located behind the first storage hanger. Bill unlocked the door and flipped a light switch.

The hanger was flooded in light, and the first thing Scotty saw was the Bonanza with its nose touching the back wall of the building, as though it had been a bad plane and was being punished by its parent. There must have been at least a quarter inch of dust on its wings and tail surfaces. This was a factory original. No paint on the aluminum skin and three cabin windows. It was an older model then his Bonanza.

Scotty walked around it, slowly, then turned to Bill and asked, "Do you think the engine will start? Is it flyable?"

"It was flown in here, but that was six years ago. It hasn't been flown since. The last time the engine was started was at least three years ago."

"Let me think about this one overnight. Right now, let's go back to your office. I'll need some additional information and the prices of the planes I'm interested in."

An hour later, Scotty had made a deal on ten of the twelve aircraft he wanted. Bill had given him a price on the Bonanza. It was a good price, but the plane would need a lot of work and would have to be disassembled and brought back to Flying Cloud in the trailer. If he made the deal, it would be his airplane, and he would have to pay Buster and Stooge to drive out here to pick it up.

That evening, Scotty called Ted in Chicago and made arrangements to have the ten planes picked up. When he had completed that conversation, he called Grace to tell her about the Bonanza and what he wanted to do. She agreed with his plan and told him they could afford to do it. *Now that I've made up my mind to buy this older model Bonanza, what am I going to do with both of them? I know that by the time I finish rebuilding this old new one I probably won't want to part with either of them,* Scotty thought.

The following morning, Scotty asked Bill, "At this time of year, are you able to keep your shop busy?"

"Not really. We have some work but it's a time for cleanup and major overhauls. This year, we aren't that busy. Why do you ask?"

"Because, if I buy that old Bonanza from you, it would have to be disassembled and shipped back to our place. So, here's my deal to you. I'll buy the plane if you'll take the wings off, remove the tail assembly, pull the engine and make a wooden cradle to support the fuselage and one to pack the engine in. I'll pay for the materials to build the cradle and the engine box if you'll have your people do the disassembly. Then, when you're ready, I'll send two of my people with a trailer to pick up the pieces."

Bill chuckled and said, "Scotty, you got a deal. I'll give you one better. I know a couple of guys that have some old birds. Give me a few of your business cards and I'll recommend your restoration facility. I took a long look at your plane and you did a great job. You made a great plane better."

Now it was Scotty's turn to smile. "Thanks a lot. I happen to think like you. I love to fly her and do every time I get the chance."

Some time later that morning, after going over some of the Bonanza disassembly details, Scotty moved on to the next stop in his quest for flying inventory.

On the last day of his successful buying trip, Scotty landed in Chicago and parked the Bonanza on the ramp at Gillette Flight Service. As long as he was this close, he wanted to stop and see Nancy. He hadn't had an opportunity to visit with her for some time now. Not since Aircraft Unlimited had opened their own service facility.

As usual, Nancy had a smart greeting for him. "Well, look who's here. Hello, hot shot. Long time no see. Are you slumming today?"

"Not really, I just came in from Joliet. Grace told me she needed a small twin-engine jet for a South American client. Chicago sold my Lear right out from under me and we didn't have anything to sell him, so I bought the Joliet Lear, along with eighteen other planes. Ted is in the process of bringing them all back here to get them ready to sell. I just thought I'd stop and visit for a few minutes before flying back to the farm."

"You're not planning to fly back today are you?"

"Well, yeah I am. Why not?"

"Because the weather forecast is predicting dense fog by this afternoon, that's why," Nancy commented.

"The sun's shining and there's no wind. The weather's great. Look outside. We finally have some warm weather, a big relief from the icebox of last week. Remember, I'm only ninety minutes from home in the Bonanza."

"I remember that your Bonanza isn't equipped for instrument flying either. What are you, stupid or do you have a death wish? Why are you in such a big hurry?"

"I'm not stupid and I don't have a death wish, Nancy. I just don't believe this fog will move that fast. I've got at least three hours according to the weather people. I don't believe the fog will pose a problem for me. Besides, Grace told me that my son Billy is sick, and the doctor wants to put him in the hospital. I need to get back today. My wife and son need my support."

Nancy looked at him with a blistering scowl and said, "So, fly commercial and get home safely. You're no good to either your wife or your firstborn if you crash that beautiful plane of yours."

CHAPTER TWENTY-SEVEN

SCOTTY'S HEAD CAME UP AND HE LOOKED AROUND the area and the clearing. At least what he could see of it. It was still dark. His hand moved up to his mouth and he wiped his lips. "Thirsty," he said. He shook his head as if to clear his vision. "Dizzy. Got to . . . stay awake . . . go to sleep I may not . . . wake up."

He reached out and scraped some snow into his hand and put some in his mouth. He moved very slowly. His strength was beginning to run out. "Very tired. I need to . . . keep going." His hand didn't seem to work well. He was having trouble opening the pistol's chamber. Finally it popped open and he loaded another cartridge. He lifted it toward the sky and pulled the trigger. The night blossomed with light.

The radio in the cockpit came to life again. Scotty's head slowly dropped to his chest and his eyes closed again. "We can see the flare. We can't be more than a mile away from the crash site."

"Roger, search team. We have an ambulance on the way to your area of search."

Scotty wasn't asleep this time but he was having a problem making out what was said. *Someone must be looking for me. I think they said something about seeing that last flare. I don't know how long I can stay awake.*

A few moments passed and his head came up again and he began coughing and retching at the same time. Liquid came flying out of his mouth and splattered his hand and the flare pistol lying in his lap. "I think . . . I heard someone say they . . . could see my flare. I hope I wasn't . . . dreaming. I'm bleeding internally . . . again. Pain . . . going away . . . dizzy . . . cold. Must be—getting close . . . to losing. Got to try . . . radio again."

He moved his good hand toward the microphone that rested on his lap. When he picked it up, it slipped out of his hand. It was covered in blood. He tried to wipe off the blood using snow and the sleeping bag covering his legs. Slowly, he picked it up and brought it to his lips, and in a voice barely above a whisper, "Mayday . . . mayday . . . one, victor down . . . need help . . . soon. Does anyone hear me? Please . . . answer."

He retched again and brought up more blood. This time not as much but it had a foamy consistency. Once again his head dropped and his eyes closed. His body began to tremble and his topcoat slid off his shoulders. His eyes opened and he tried to get the coat back over his shoulders. It became a chore because of his trembling. It kept sliding off as quickly as he put it back onto his shoulders. Finally, frustrated and with tears of defeat slipping down his cheeks, he let it stay in his lap.

Once again he looked for the microphone, found it under his coat by pulling on the cable. He lifted it to his lips and this time he managed to push the send button. "Mayday . . . mayday . . . one victor down . . . I need help . . . soon. Does . . . anyone hear me?"

"Bonanza three, two, one one, victor, this is C.A.P. Seneca five, seven, pop, over."

He began crying as he pulled the microphone back to his mouth. "Five seven pop, this is one . . . victor. I'm down . . . on the edge of a clearing . . . the fuselage of . . . the plane . . . is in the trees. Wings should be visible s-s-somewhere near the tree line. You should be able to follow the . . . debris right to me. I'm bleeding, I think—both legs are broken . . . very cold."

"One Victor. We have your beacon, and are homing in on you. Can you control your bleeding? Over."

"Seven pop . . . thanks for being there. I've made some bad landings . . . in my day, but . . . this is the first time I can't walk away from one. I'm doing my best . . . to control . . . bleeding, but . . . I'm so cold . . . dizzy . . . tired. Having . . . problems staying awake. I hear your engine. You're close . . . OH, THANK GOD!"

"One victor, there is a rescue team just a few miles away from you. They should be there soon. Do you think you can hold out until the ground team can reach you?"

No answer was heard. He tried a second time and then a third. Still there was nothing. "Alex flight service, this is Seneca, five, seven, pop, pilot of downed plane has apparently passed out. Please contact ground party and ask them to fire a flare so I can guide them to the clearing. I'm circling the clearing now and I can see some debris on the ground. To save some time, scramble the chopper."

"Five-seven pop, Alex control. The chopper has been scrambled. They should be airborne in ten or fifteen minutes. The ground team says they can see you circling.

"Roger, Alex. I see them now."

With those words the pilot of five seven pop dived his plane toward the wreckage and pulled up quickly. He flew over the ground team and directly to the wreckage. The ground team waved and began running across the clearing. The first man across was at least seventy-five yards ahead of the rest of the team. He quickly weaved his way through the trees and slid to a stop at Scotty's side. "Scotty, Scotty, it's me Stooge. Are you all right?" While he babbled to him, Stooge checked for a pulse and waved to the team just arriving. "He's alive but he's hurt bad. Bring the stretcher over here. We need to get him off the ground.

Buster looked down at Scotty with tears in his eyes. He dropped to his knees next to him and said, "Hey, hotshot, we're here. We found you and we'll take good care of you. Our team is Aircraft Unlimited. Don Kopinski, Frank Ross, and Ted were on their way back to Chicago after delivering that DC6 when they heard you were down and they diverted to our place. We couldn't let you down because you never let us down."

Frank had been a helicopter evacuation pilot in Korea. He knew first aid and he carried the large first aid kit. He knelt down beside Scotty and waved an ammonia ampoule under his nose. When Scotty's eyes popped open, Frank said, "Scotty, we need to get you onto this stretcher. We'll be lifting you but we need to know about any broken bones. We don't want to cause you any further damage."

"I'm not . . . dreaming, am I? You, you guys are all real . . . aren't you?"

"Yes, Scotty. We're real. We finally found you, with your help and a whole lot of others," Frank responded.

About that time, the cockpit radio came to life, "Seneca, five, seven, pop, this is Air Rescue One. ETA is four minutes. Please turn on your landing lights and high intensity strobe. Over."

"Roger, air rescue one, strobes and lights are on."

"Seneca, five, seven, pop, we have a visual. What shape is the pilot in? Over."

"Air rescue one, he has broken bones, bleeding, apparently in shock. He passed out on me a few minutes ago. The ground search team is there now. They should have him ready for you by the time you land. Over."

"Roger, five, seven, pop, we have the wreckage in sight. Thanks for your help, and great job finding him so quickly. Congratulations. We'll take it from here. With the ground team's help, we should have him ready to transport in a few minutes."